**Green
Of
Each
Window**

Green
of
Each
Window

The Immortal,

Magical,

Dionysian

Act of Inhabiting

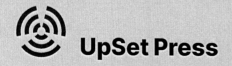

UpSet Press

PO Box 200340
Brooklyn, NY 11220

upsetpress.org

Green Of Each Window:
The Immortal, Magical, Dionysian Act of Inhabiting

—

Special thanks to Sue Chan, Reference Librarian at National Library of Australia, for providing Nicole Brossard text (i.e. quote on p.14) in original French.

UpSet Press is an independent, not-for-profit (501c3 tax exempt) organization advancing thought-provoking works of literature, including translated works, to promote curiosity/transformation, i.e., to upset the status quo.

—   —

ISBN 978-1-937357-83-2
Library of Congress Control Number:
2022942905
Printed in US

Book and cover design by
Jessica D'Elena-Tweed

Contents

NOTE
ON

ACCOMPANYING
SONGS

Each work is paired with a song.
The songs are not meant as musical backdrops.

They exist as extensions of the works, echoes.
They run parallel to the works but not in real time, not in sync.

Like a soundtrack for a film but not the score.
They're offered as imprints, signage, marginalia.

They engage the reader's eyes, and
infer an audio context off the page.

It's recommended to listen to the songs,
either while reading the works, or after, or in clusters.

The relationship between work and song varies.
In some instances, a song may offer backstory,

postscript, an ironic juxtaposition,
an exclamation mark, a punch line, hymn or hook.

All the songs are listed in the playlists
they were sourced from in the back matter.

Ah me

E vero

(It's real)   (This is real life)

(This is a photograph of real life)

(This is the only chance you will have at real life)

—Cole Swensen, *"Oh"*

Feu Adonis

Parenthesis = In a Mezzo-Soprano Voice, Moi, The Narrator

Since Adonis is dead,
the reader may forgive him,

speak of him semi-fondly,
recount his loves without rebuke,

avow the following saga,
The Adonis Saga, as not immoral.

Instead, one should recite it,
project it in one's mind

with one's own cast,
melodramatically, without judgement.

And since parts of it are impossible
to act out in real life,

one should surrender to its illogic,
unless, of course, one can animate it.

Meanwhile, the playlists can easily be recreated
to put one in the apartment of Adonis,

my foremost crush.

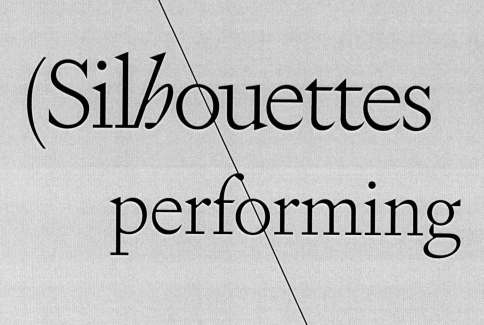

(Silhouettes

performing

rhythmic gymnastics)

Cast of Characters

Adonis,

Nico,

Thaïs,

composites, the three of them:

Adonis in the world of the sonnet,

Nico in the world of the hourglass and the vinyl ice bucket,

Thaïs in the world of the open balcony.

Adonis,

Nico,

Thaïs,

running, the three of them:

Adonis in the world of mythology and starfish,

Nico in the world of the red line and French new wave,

Thaïs in the world of lakes and the express bus.

Adonis,

Nico,

Thaïs,

masked, the three of them:

Adonis in a track suit, on a rooftop,

Nico at carnival, in a masquerade mask, floating,

Thaïs, in the lungs, in the colony, in the folds of a summer dress.

Adonis,

Nico,

Thaïs,

undressed in these pages, the three of them:

three Christs of the Abyss,

three private dancers,

three crude collages in the Byzantine style.

The Devil,
Adonis,
close friends, the two of them:
with butterflies of the restless,
with books dog-eared from quoting, passed between them like a joint,
with the attentiveness of virgins at a saturnalia,
through the blues of brownstones where prudes spy on their lovemaking.

Ellen, Richard—The Two Beasts:
Adonis saw them consuming his spawn,
massaging their plump throats with lines for a new coda,
for a stage with mirrors and incense to conceal their odiousness,
for his funeral and his fortieth day mass,
for his post, and his thumb drive of presentations,
for his absence to be filled in with wet concrete,
for his digital tombstone with a picture of the three of them smiling.

Roach,
Rich Man,
God,
Enzo,
Business Man,
Lady in Fine Hat,
in supporting roles:
riding turbulent swells
and refracting light
into the infected nuclei of black holes.

With guest appearances by Olga Broumas,
Federico García Lorca,
Bob Marley, and the glare.

(Adonis removes a couple of condoms from his desk drawer, which he deftly slides into his side pocket. He closes the drawer, and logs off his computer. Standing up, he scans his cubicle to see if he is forgetting anything. He rubs his finger where his wedding band would be—if he were wearing it. Still, he feels it on his finger. So, he rubs the area to assure himself of its absence. Also, he enjoys touching the silky skin where it once gripped him. He sidesteps around his chair before tucking it in, and then saunters out of the office.)

Une voix d'homme quelque part dans l'hôtel disait un poème dans une langue étrangère. Ma première impression fut qu'il discutait.

—Nicole Brossard, *"NOUVELLE OPTIQUE"*

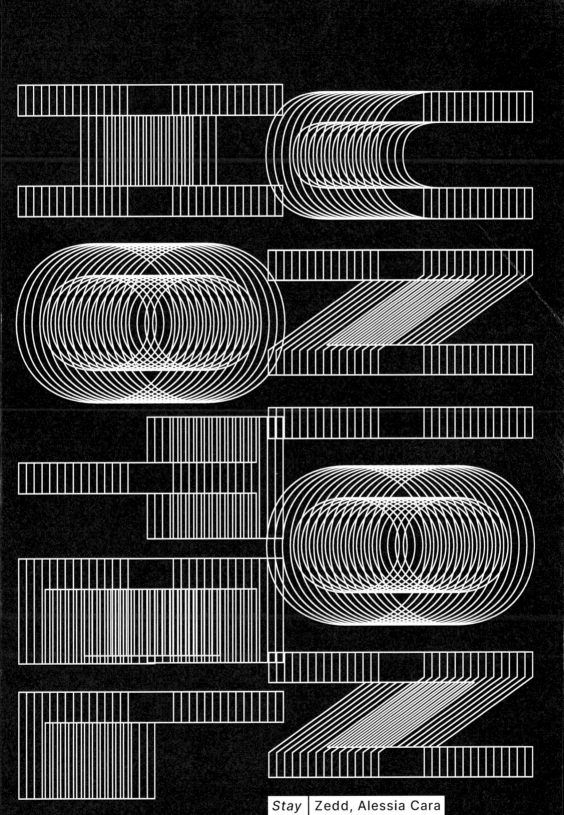

Stay | Zedd, Alessia Cara

ROOF	<<<<<<<<	IT WOULD REDEEM US	>>>>>>>>	ROOF
12	Totem	^ ^ ^	It Would Have Soul	12
11	Narrative	^ ^	Our Cancers	11
10	Organic	^ ^	Seeds of Things	10
9	Turbulence	^ ^	Hollows of Sky	9
8	Most Quoted	^ ^	Keats	8
7	No Fear	^ ^	How It Would Feel	7
6	Fucking	^ ^	Our Aplomb	6
5	Greektown	^ ^	The Lyrics	5
4	Karma	^ ^	Jealousy	4
3	Spatial Poetics	^ ^	Texture	3
2	Ten Years	^ ^	This Moment	2
1	Oblivion	^ ^ ^	Its Gravity	1
GROUND	>>>>>>>>	ENTRANCE	<<<<<<<<	GROUND

No Judgment	Niall Horan

This is Real Life

Tonight You Might | Synthia, Lady Wray

There are certain things Adonis doesn't want to admit,
not even to himself.
With eyes burning, he searches for starfish—
his childhood in Coney Island.

It's the honeymoon suite tonight.
The honeymoon might last all of one hour—
an early check-in/checkout,
please/thank you.

In Union Hotel, there are two kinds of lewdness.
One naïve. One sophisticated.
The first is shameful.
The second a secret happiness.

Thaïs describes Adonis as someone who is already handsome
losing ugliness. Nico describes him as safe.

Surveillance cameras undulate at the ends of hallways,
granulating the three protagonists, timestamping
their arrivals and departures, neither sober
nor drunk. Doors click shut quietly.

**(Silhouette
of roach)**

Forthcoming

When they placed the word *Forthcoming* after the title, I fully understood the incommunicability of my innocence. I could not go back and undo anything I had done or written, nor did I want to. I called them fictions, but my friends recognized themselves, and disowned me. It could have been worse. They could have sued. But any percentage of zero is still zero. That much math I remember. Apparently, I am the zero. And all those who come into contact with me are transfigured also to zero. Not an Adonis after all.

After the terrible thing happened at work—not that the thing itself was terrible—but afterward, what happened, the response to the thing, that was terrible! I hated going to work and all the eyes looking away, judging me. My bosses would meet secretly, daily, to grope their own terrible largeness. They did this for eighteen months, then they called me into their office. They said their bosses wanted to meet me, and that I should not mention the terrible thing. Ha! I laughed involuntarily. The terrible thing had become a weapon—my weapon!

They were then, because of the full moon, in a trance. I perceived them as two beasts waiting for me.

1. I could hide, or
2. I could run away, or
3. I could confront them.

If I did nothing, if I maintained my gait, I would bump into them. So, I hid for a moment, behind a lamppost, then I second-guessed my hiding spot and my hiding in general. Best to confront them, I convinced myself. I quickly rehearsed what I would say if they said this or that, then I resumed my approach. But when I perceived myself, walking towards them with a limp—I turned around and ran! It was the first time I ran in years. And I felt the worst joy.

They broke the bed fucking, then I sat on the bed and, there being no other space to sit, she sat next to me. The bed tilted like a creaky seesaw. I said, Wait. She said, Why, why wait? And why are you whispering? She smiled demonically. Because you are no longer real, and you are consuming me. Can you hear me? I unexpectedly became aware I was lying in a bed with a roach in a hotel in a city that was being devoured by roaches. I wasn't dying or dreaming, I was becoming, in a zero-sum game of passion, the roach.

There being no easeful melody or soundtrack to the forgiveness I needed, no space in the hotel that was safe to receive or store (let alone nourish) any mercy, I couldn't bear the degree of my deceit. The thoroughness of it could not be wholly inventoried. There was no longer any enjoyment in it. The sneaking around became a trapdoor I fell into, bottomless. Falling into is the cruelty. Bottomless is its kindness. Why do I only love a little? Or fleetingly? Why do I love less than I am loved? Is love a zero-sum game of passion? Is less-than-half-in-love the real hell?

There's no other woman, but there's always the yearning for another woman. I consume my own yearning as a means of self-control, self-cannibalism. It plagues me. My first scream is at the first sign of a symptom. It is then all the sighs of past orgasms are erased from my memory, washed away by an enormous wave of anxiety. I no longer see myself as the roach. I now see myself, in the tiniest piece of mirror, in the convex base of a bedside lamp, eating the roach. The nausea that overwhelms me is a reprieve from my own terrible largeness.

I, a childish man, am lost in a hotel. I ride an elevator up and down. This elevator only goes to certain floors. The wrong floors. I follow an illogical numbering system in a maze of corridors. This place is a series of NO EXITs, DO NOT DISTURBs. Take away the carnal component of a hotel and it's nothing more than a terminal for somnambulists. There's no enjoyment in the visitation. I sensed this when I walked out of the elevator and through the lobby. I also sensed they could smell the sex on me. I am the contagion. I exited a side entrance which was attached to a coffee shop. I bought a coffee which I used to warm my hands. Then I walked into the snow. And even the snow avoided my touch.

Goodbye. Help! Love is the experience of a vulnerability greater than flying. Love tolerates the unbearable. My hip is killing me, and I have no one to pick me up from the airport. This is how I decide what cities to visit. In this very instant I am waiting for my baggage, regularly shifting my weight from leg to leg. In a few minutes I will be sitting in a passenger seat, looking out a window at an unfamiliar landscape. I will receive its strangeness as if I am being flirted with. (I delude myself, yes.) As I smile, the driver will ask, "How long are you existing?" I will reply, "The glass broke on the flight." Neither of us is from here. But I trust she knows where she's going.

When the moment is no longer forthcoming, I feel a loss. This is why I prefer foreplay to sex. This is why I write more than I live. In writing, I can postpone, I can push back, I can delay. In living, I have no control. Things happen to me all the time. When things happen to me, they deplete or disturb my desire. And I am mainly my desire:

> 1. The desire to be loved, not by everyone all at once, but by everyone a little at a time, sequentially.
> 2. The desire to transform the erotic into a religious experience—which is different than a spiritual experience, which the erotic already is. A religious experience is distinct in that it assigns a tender choreography, a sacred currency to acts.
> 3. The desire to undress in front of a stranger, and to stand before her naked. In that moment, looking at her look at my nakedness, I have to fight back orgasm. Such is my sensitivity.

An enormous wave, hiding in the most obvious place, waits to ambush me. I undress down to my underwear. I look up and down the beach. There's no one else here, no one within a thousand yards. It's mid October and it's my birthday. I left work early to come here for a swim. The absence of people terrifies me. The wind is howling, and the sand is pelting my skin. Also, there are these strange gnats, half-alive, mixed in with the sand that I keep having to spit out of my mouth. I wade into the water slowly, carefully. It's low tide and there are many hidden sandbars, I know. If I break my neck here, now, I'm done. I walk out a hundred—two hundred yards. I'm still only waist deep. My feet are going numb from the cold. There are goosebumps on my arms and chest. "I am asking a question," I say aloud as I take off my underwear. A simple "Yes" followed by a "?".

We'll never forget so and so, they say. The husband who cheated and died of guilt. The father who sacrificed everything and died of exhaustion. The artist who lived a double-life and died of tension, works uncompleted. The best dive bar in Brooklyn, the best Chinese restaurant in Chinatown, our first apartment, etcetera, etcetera. They couch their memories in fondness. Then I come and crawl on their couch. I am the zero in their sea of nostalgia. They don't want me here. They don't want to be reminded of my existence. They want me dead already, or if not dead, gone. But my death (and my arrival) is eternally forthcoming.

MALBEC

What's Your Pleasure? | Jessie Ware

(Adonis knocks on a door. The door opens.)

ADONIS: Hello.

NICO: (Peeking out from behind the door) Oh, it's you.

ADONIS:(Entering the room) Yes. Thank you for seeing me.

NICO: (Closing the door behind him) My handsome swimmer. You are taller than I expected.

ADONIS: I brought you a bottle of wine, and also coffee from Jamaica, and a book of poems.

NICO: Is the coffee picked by child slaves?

ADONIS: No. No. It's from...a Japanese company. They bought the mountain.

ROACH: Liar!

ADONIS: What did you say?

ROACH: You have the face of a liar.

ADONIS: Look who's talking. Your face is flat as a wall, and your voice is like two rocks rubbing together. (Nico snorts)

ROACH: Are you a man? Or a squid?

ADONIS: I don't understand.

ROACH: I've known Nico, your mistress, for a long time. I was a roach in her house, but to tell you the truth, I prefer hotels to houses. It's the surfaces. They're smooth and clutter-free. I feel like I'm ice skating. Ha, ha, ha! Have you ever skated on a lake? On black ice no less! Nobody knows how much frozen lakes frighten me. Skating on a lake is very scary. Oh, it's incredibly scary when the ice cracks. If you go through the ice, you don't stand a chance. Even if you catch yourself halfway, it's near impossible to pull yourself out. The cold water causes all your muscles to restrict and lock, and your legs, your legs weigh a ton. Those damned legs! (Nico takes off her leggings.)

ADONIS: I'm not interested in ice skating.

ROACH: You're missing my point.

ADONIS: For God's sake, shut up!

ROACH: (Mocking) For God's sake? (Serious) God is a stupidity.

(Adonis heard "stupidity" as "stupid head". He glanced at the roach because "stupid head" is what his daughter says.)

RICH MAN: (In the window) My, my, looky here. I didn't expect to see you.

ROACH: He likes to sneak around. (Laughing) Do you remember how he used to come over after you went to work, and seduce your niece, the virgin?

RICH MAN: How could I forget?

ADONIS: (To Rich Man) She was so unlike you.

RICH MAN: You should leave now.

ADONIS: I'll leave when I'm done.

ROACH: Don't be rude. This is his hotel. We are the visitors here.

ADONIS: I am paying for my visit. He is doing me no kindness or favor.

ROACH: He is magnanimous to accept your money. He doesn't need your business.

ADONIS: If you don't shut up, I'll squash you!

ROACH: Ha, ha, ha! Everyone thinks they can squash me, but few have the courage to try it. You? You don't have the courage, or the strength of stomach, that much I know.

ADONIS: (Irritated) I didn't come here to argue with you.

ROACH: Why did you come here?

ADONIS: (Softening) For Nico. To be with Nico.

ROACH: Well, don't mind me then.

ADONIS: The worst thing in the world is a roach. (He turns to Nico.)

NICO: I never know how to initiate.

ADONIS: You're more beautiful in person.

NICO: Beautiful?

ADONIS: Yes.

NICO: I get 'cute' a lot.

ADONIS: No, not cute. But you do look older in your photos.

NICO: Really? Is that ok?

ADONIS: Yes, of course.

NICO: (Letting her hair down) Do you like my hair? I always had short hair. I'm not used to this mane.

(Nico climbs onto Adonis' lap and starts kissing him.)

UNBORN CHILD 1: I will be born with big eyes. They will reflect more than they will see. I will marry the first man I sleep with.

UNBORN CHILD 2: I will be born with a cleft. No one will look at me. I will commit suicide before my sixteenth birthday. By drowning. They will not find the body.

ROACH: Your children?

ADONIS: My poor children...

UNBORN CHILD 3: I will be born perfectly healthy from an easeful labor. My eyes will be blue as an LA sky.

RICH MAN: What do you know of LA?

UNBORN CHILD 3: I know the dreams of all the children there. I know their thirst. Anyway, (to Adonis) you will tell the doctors to circumcise me, and I will die from the surgery.

UNBORN CHILD 4: Such whiners! The lot of them. I will be born blind and deaf. And I will become the world's greatest mathematician.

(Nico twists off Adonis and removes her sweater in a singular motion. She takes one step backwards, then sits on the other bed, naked, facing him. He undresses and goes to her. They make love on top of both beds.)

NICO: Is this too rough?

ADONIS: No, no. It's perfect.

UNBORN CHILD 5: I will be born in four places at once: 1. in a field. 2. in a desert. 3. on a mountain. 4. on a rooftop. I will be left alone immediately. The sun, with her manicured fingers, will reach down and tickle me. But, then...the night...and its swarm of mosquitoes.

UNBORN CHILD 6: I will be born a clone of my mother. Like her, I will grow strong and beautiful. Like her, I will fight back many monsters. Like her, the monsters will name me: Witch, Whore. Whatever. As they speak, I will rip out their tongues.

RICH MAN: No child should speak so violently. Are you not nestled in your mother's womb?

ROACH: The child speaks the truth. I've seen the future. It's more violent than you can imagine.

RICH MAN: The future is for the poor.

ADONIS: (Sighing) My poor children...

ROACH: (Sadly) Your poor children...

(Nico and Adonis collapse side by side on the bed. They had made tender love under the eyes of Roach and Rich Man.)

RICH MAN: Nico?

NICO: (Furious) What?

RICH MAN: Come back to me. I'll take care of you.

NICO: No. You are just a meme, and nothing more. Besides, you are ugly, your hands feel like sandpaper, from obsessively counting money, and I don't believe in marriage. I love my freedom too much, the liberty to choose who I see, where I go, what I do and don't do. I love my ever-evolving self, the choice to change appearances, change opinions, change lovers. You would imprison me. You would reduce me to a maid, or worse, a supervisor of maids. (She puts her hands on Adonis' chest) I like him. He does gentle well.

RICH MAN: You witch. You whore.

UNBORN CHILDREN: Mama. Papa. Mama. Mama.

ADONIS: (Awakening) She can't hear you. She can't hear you.

UNBORN CHILD 2: Papa, I want the surgery. (Bursting into tears) Oh Papa, I want the surgery so bad!

The Squid

You Know How to Make Me Feel so Good | Susan Cadogan

Can I kiss the squid?
I will kiss the squid
I kiss the squid

Can I glean its ink?
I will glean its ink
I glean its ink

Can I paint the squid?
I will paint the squid
I paint the squid

This squid I painted
I could not have painted
before I kissed you

My Darling

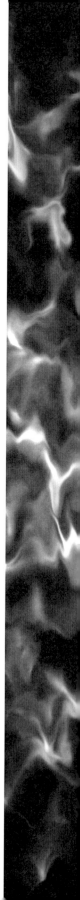

Beautiful | Qveen Herby

You never say 'My Heart!'
or 'My Love!'
or 'Ma Chérie!'

You prefer to say 'My Cock!'
'Take It!'
'Suck it!'

Oh yes, there's also 'Oh Fuck!'
'I'm Coming!'
finishing yourself with your hand.

You look for what's imperfect
in your attraction,
in your submission to lovers.

You play back scenes in your head.
You obsess over the imperfections.
They get you so fucking hard!

SIRENS

Dive In | Trey Songz

(Rooftop)

SIRENS: Whoop! Whoop!

(The Devil and Thaïs are inflating a blow-up pool with an electric air pump at the golden hour.)

DEVIL: God's dogs are out tonight.

THAÏS: Weren't you, once, one of his dogs? His most notorious?

DEVIL: No. Never a dog. I'm a full-blooded wolf.

THAÏS: Wolf. Dog. What's the difference?

DEVIL: Hmph. Dogs can be trained.

(They finish inflating the pool. Enter Adonis.)

SIRENS: Whoop! Whoop!

ADONIS: Who let the dogs out? Woof! Woof!

DEVIL: Who let the dogs out? Woof! Woof!

SIRENS: Whoop! Whoop!

THAÏS: Animals. Both of you.

(They embrace. The Devil lines the pool with a couple of blankets.)

ADONIS: (Laughing) What's this? I didn't bring my bathing suit. But I did bring gifts. A book for you (to the Devil)—Lorca's 'Barbarous Nights.'

DEVIL: Oh man, I was there. I lived it.

ADONIS: I know you did. And for you (to Thaïs)—Rigoberto González's 'So Often the Pitcher Goes to Water until It Breaks.'

THAÏS: Thank you. I don't have anything for you.

ADONIS: That's OK. That's what makes it a gift. I didn't expect anything.

(Thaïs kisses Adonis.)

DEVIL: Aw...

ADONIS: But if I knew you were going to kiss me...

DEVIL: You demigod, you.

THAÏS: Huh?

DEVIL: Adonis is a centaur. Half man, half horse.

ADONIS: From the waist down, all horse.

DEVIL: The Androcephalous Syndrome.

THAÏS: (To Adonis) So, not a wolf? Like him.

ADONIS: No, I wish! What about you?

THAÏS: I'm a saint. Can't you tell? (Thaïs curtsies.)

ADONIS: A saint?

DEVIL: (Lifting a bottle of champagne) No one wants to be a saint anymore. It requires dying.

THAÏS: A saint is just another word for martyr.

DEVIL: (Nudging the cork) Or suicide bomber.

ADONIS: Or deluded victim.

THAÏS: Or mother. (The Devil kneels and kisses her feet. Adonis kneels and hugs her thigh.) Yes, it's true. I'm a poor substitute for god.

DEVIL: (Rising) Saints are for those who lack the capacity to evolve.

ADONIS: (To Thaïs) But you're alive, and healthy. (Massaging her thigh) You ran a marathon yesterday.

(Thaïs lifts Adonis. Then she pulls down her collar with her index figure, revealing, between her cleavage, a gaping wound in her chest.)

ADONIS: Owe.

(Thaïs takes Adonis' hand and places it over her wound.)

DEVIL: (Popping the cork) Champagne?

SIRENS: Whoop! Whoop!

THAÏS: Absolutely, yes.

(Adonis removes his hand.)

DEVIL: (Gulping) It goes down easily. (He hands the bottle to Thaïs.)

THAÏS: I was dying of thirst. (Gulping) Thank you. (She hands the bottle to Adonis.)

ADONIS: (Gulping) What happened? (He hands the bottle to the Devil.)

THAÏS: It's a long story.

(They all climb into the pool.)

Hallelujah

I'm The Man, That Will Find You | Connan Mockasin

I fell into an elastic happiness
There's sensitivity in my deceit

I've lost friends I've lost lovers
I don't understand their visits

The world is made of gasps and amens
I like when others react audibly

How do I translate? A tone?
There are thousands of others like me

I sometimes think I belong to someone else
This alarms me because I'm afraid of disappearing

And no one notices my absence
I live in a kind of purgatory

I make gestures that are unobserved
Or considered obscene when observed

I'm a squid and a tree
My happiness comes from the deepest darkness

I expand or shrink in proportion to one's mouth
A drop for every sigh every hallelujah

Broumas

Dopamine | BØRNS

In dreams whose sex I cannot control,
I follow Olga Broumas into the ocean:

a novice diver exploring a shark reef.

How many nights I slept with her—
and she doesn't even know I exist.

How many nights I slept with her—
my wife and children slept beside me.

I should be arrested for my transgressions.
I'm not this brave in person.

On the page I never panic, never lack
confidence. I'm always, you know, sexy.

Octopi emit a cloud of ink when they sense danger.
Broumas' poems are octopi inside my brain,

exploding ink everywhere,
burning my eyes, turning my gaze back.

O..., I try calling out,
but no sound comes from my mouth—

just bubbles. Perfect little o's
I see above my drowning.

EARTH

Alles ist gut | PA Sports

(Sidewalk café)

ENZO: (Smoking) This city is built on the ruins of the previous city, and the previous city on the one before it, and the city before that one also built on the ruins of the city before it, and so on, going back thousands of years. So, it shouldn't surprise you they outlawed any type of excavation, anywhere in the city, (he ashes on the sidewalk) for fear the slightest disturbance could lead to a massive collapse.

ADONIS: (Sipping his coffee) When you build on rubble, you shouldn't kick at the foundation, eh?

ENZO: (Looking up at the sky) Still, I like to think with each new city we are a little closer to the stars. This is happening all over the world, everywhere you look. The earth is expanding, layer on layer, section by section, like a balloon, a giant hot air balloon. Have you ever seen them blow up a giant hot air balloon?

ADONIS: No. What are you getting at?

ENZO: The earth.

ADONIS: The earth?

ENZO: Yeah, the earth. Once the size of a moon, now swollen (he mimics holding up a large bosom, with cigarette between his fingers) with the breast milk of the stillborn.

The Children

L-O-V-E – Long Version | Joss Stone

The children I did not born—
These too are my children!

Each one a hand
the doctors cut off. (Hand/bird.)

They don't hesitate, my children,
they fly away!

Now I stand outside, the sun on my wrists,
naked in front of a new lover.

I squeeze invisible fists.
Open, close. (Open/close.)

The body does not forget.
It tastes air once and holds its breath.

They can have my hands,
those fleshy stars. My children—

I carry their teeth in my breast.

The Snakes and the Lilies

I oppose the snakes and the lilies
of the airways and the highways

I protest the secular state the common states
and the statesmen of the secular state

I interrupt the adulterous and the vainglorious
I carry on my shoulder a hunting rifle

I carry the sorrow and the guilt of the figurative
and the real the literal Germans

I donate my liver to the alcoholic the homeless
the Jew and the Muslim

I restore to the afflicted their voilà
their memory and their forgetting

I forgive the gatekeeper and the prison guard
the doorman and the pimp

I dress up the undressed children of disease
of drowned parents of forests of myth

I wipe the semen from the lips of prostitutes
and place the Eucharist on their tongues

I comb back the wild hair of heathens
so I may look upon them and kiss their cheeks

I doubt the innocence and indifference of nature
my god is a spiteful god a ninja god

I gather all the loose arms and legs from the battlefield
and sew them onto the wounded of my side

RICHARD

(Office)

ADONIS: (Hovering in doorway) Hey.

RICHARD: Come in, come in.

ADONIS: New office, huh?

RICHARD: Dude, yeah, they gave me this. Can you believe it? It's bigger than I thought. Just look at all these bookshelves.

ADONIS: (Scanning the empty shelves) I see.

RICHARD: No books though—that's what you're thinking. I see it in your face. I'm an expert at reading people. It's one of my talents, reading the room. As theater director on the side, I have to do that all the time. That, and solving problems. I'm a problem-solver. Some people like to harp and criticize, be negative. That's all they do. You know what I mean? They just want to find fault. It's easy to find fault. It's hard to fix things. I don't want to hear about problems. It just brings me down. I'm all about solutions, moving on, you know. (Richard pauses, and motions Adonis to sit. Adonis sits down.) And that's what I want to talk to you about.

ADONIS: Ok.

RICHARD: My promotion is official now.

ADONIS: I see. Congrats.

RICHARD: But you didn't send me a congratulatory reply.

ADONIS: I just congratulated you.

RICHARD: Hm. Well, I'm glad to hear that, thank you. You know, this whole promotion thing took way longer than I expected, than anyone expected. Years from when it was promised to me. All the paperwork, and justification letters. You wouldn't believe how many times we had to submit and resubmit paperwork. I almost walked away from it all. It wasn't worth the hassle, I said. But Ellen wanted me—needed me to stick it out. I was ready to go do theater full time. We're doing a big production of *Ragtime* this summer.

ADONIS: Oh.

RICHARD: You do know *Ragtime*, yes?

ADONIS: No.

RICHARD: It's a classic. Really, you should see it. Actually, let me ask you this. The n-word is in the script, and not just once here and there, it's in there quite often. Yeah man. It was that time, you know. I wanted to keep it real, so I left it in. I feel like the decision was mine to make. The producers wanted to take it out, to change it. But I didn't want to. I needed to be true to the script, to the time, you know. Let me ask you, what would you do?

ADONIS: I wouldn't use it.

RICHARD: I don't know, dude. I think you might.

ADONIS: No, I'm certain.

RICHARD: Well, I left it in. And the producers are very worried about the whole thing. But I told them, it had to stay. It's history! I'm an artist. This isn't some college class. It's for real, you know.

ADONIS: Ok. But I wouldn't.

RICHARD: Eh, well, water under the bridge. (Richard takes off his glasses) I'm surprised by your answer.

ADONIS: I don't know why.

RICHARD: I thought—I mean, (he puts his glasses back on) I know you're a writer and all. So, I figured, you know, you'd put language first, be true to the word.

ADONIS: I find no redeemable truth in that word.

RICHARD: What about the notion of reclaiming that word, and all its nega-tive-ness, and using it as a term of endearment?

ADONIS: Is that how you used it?

RICHARD: Anyway, you should see the play. Then we can talk more about it. But that's not why I called you in. I called you in to talk about my promotion. I get the sense you're not happy about it.

The Cormorant

Gemini | Knox Fortune

I fly and swim.
I upset the stillnesses in pockets
hiding from my kind:

> the kamikaze
> and orphans of the kamikaze.

I fly and swim.
I dart from mooring to mooring,
slitting anchor lines.

> Coiled on the ocean floor:
> the horizon's intestines.

I fly and swim.
I parcel murk and splendor,
forking light

> in throat's darkness.
> An aubade for each grunt.

I fly and swim.
I clasp a drowning face
in a halo of bubbles,

> taking from one world
> a corpse to bring into the next.

This Silence

Numb | Portishead

I'm walking down a flight of stairs in a dark stairwell. Because I can barely see, I feel for each step with a toe-tap before stepping down. I keep one hand on the rail. It feels like a warm pipe with hot water pulsing through. Or it's my pulse, reverberating. I can't let go. If I do, I will lose my balance. My legs ache from the slow descent. The stairwell is getting darker. I can't see my own feet, or my hand on the rail. I feel my body stretching, opening, and being squished all at the same time, as if a snake has wrapped itself around me and is squeezing me—squeezing my neck. More than a choking sensation, I feel like my head is going to pop off. I grasp for the top of my head with my free hand and push down to keep it attached to my body.

I stumble onto flat ground, falling forward, the weight of an ocean on my back. The floor is hot and broken. My hands and knees sink into its crevices. The cement crumbles and shifts under me. The more I try to push myself up, the more I sink down. A surge of electricity runs through my body, up from the floor, and throws me back onto the stairs. I reach for the rail and pull myself up further, backwards, pushing through my heels. There is an explosion of light, and now I sense my blindness is real, permanent. Everything is white, all white.

I turn, contorting myself so as not to let go of the rail, and climb back up the stairs. I climb quickly, trying to outrun my pain, my body, my blindness. I'm taking two stairs a time, tripping, banging my shins, knees, jumping back up, and scrambling up the stairs. I use the rail as a catapult, flinging myself upwards in disjointed spurts. Then, suddenly, there is no rail, there are no stairs—my body is suspended in air—in what I imagine can only be sky. The blue sky of morning.

In this suspended-ness I feel my exhaustion. And I submit to it. Slowly, casually, I feel myself fall. My vision comes back, sort of. There are grainy images that fade as if I'm being pulled away from them. There's smoke that coils like a snake. I feel myself gaining speed. There's a fire pit with lightning coming out of it. I'm gaining more speed. There's a blue sky with a blur falling through it. I must be.

This blur. I feel a great weight in my chest. I no longer feel my limbs. It's as if all my organs have turned into concrete blocks and these blocks have slid into my chest. There are others falling too. Next to me. I know they're falling next to me, with me—that we're falling together—at the same speed, because of the constancy of their screaming. That they can sustain their screaming as they fall comforts me. Protects me.

Wake up. No! Wake up. No! Wake up. No! I see myself shooting up in bed. No! Heart beating, but sighing. No! As I behold my sleeping wife. No! And child next to me. No! No! No! Don't deceive yourself. You're not waking up from this.

Their screaming stops abruptly, without warning or crescendo. Oh God. I must be. This silence.

NICO

(Room with city view)

NICO: Underground is no place for innocence. (Lightning flash) In film, it's *The Terrible Place*, (thunder clap) where the monster, sex unknown, but most often a hideous man, drags his victims to. Most often, scantily clad women, to further torture or dismember them. The victims are targeted because they're sexually active, or hyperactive. The monster personifies an STD, or an unwanted pregnancy. Because even though the monster has the face of the devil, the consequence, or the punishment, make no mistake, comes from God. The women are sluts, and the monster is a punishing God. That's the message. And there's always one woman, a virgin, who is *The Final Girl*. She stands up to the monster, and either defeats him, or escapes from him in the final scene.

ADONIS: We cheer for her.

NICO: Yeah. But no one mourns her when she dies years later, off-screen. From emphysema. Or cancer.

ADONIS: I'm no monster.

NICO: I know.

(Adonis goes down.)

ROACH: And he would go down…

NICO: Wait.

ADONIS: What is it?

NICO: It's just that, it's so intimate.

ADONIS: Yes...

NICO: Do you want to?

ADONIS: Yes! If you want.

NICO: Ok, go ahead.

(Adonis goes down.)

ROACH: He would go down, and above all, go into... Into the abandonment of all laws, into the present, into the ground, though not inside a coffin, into physical contact with the soil, into periodic fits, into heat, after long and spirited meows, intolerable, into such strong communication with the ground, the soil, into the far-off distance, intoxicated, into a portal to another instant, into a hole which one can fall, into a mirror, an empty room, into the hidden secrets of safes, into nothingness, into closed eyes, into deep breathing, into a lake, with reflections of trees, into Nico, into night, into darkness, into a mouth, and finally into the inviolable act, the performance, into the air like someone giving a bird its freedom, into a crevice in which pleasure swells, he bites into, into moon bits of light, into a cathedral, unafraid, into a large tumbler, filling up with the new night, into the innumerable nerve endings of the body, swimming in rip currents, climbing the waves of the brain, into the freckled soul, translucent, into the tiniest piece of mirror, into precision, into a volume intently moving onward, upward, into the entire night, humming, vibrating.

(The television and stage lights are turned off. Both stage and audience are in darkness... Stirring...Sighing... Quiet. Then, a giant, digital clock blinks 12:00.)

NICO: Ah, Adonis.

ADONIS: Ah, Nico.

ROACH: Twelve o'clock!

(The stage lights are turned on.)

ADONIS: (Rising) I have to go. I have something for you. (Adonis hands Nico an envelope.)

NICO: What is it?

ADONIS: (Getting dressed) Pictures. (Nico opens the envelope) Nudes. Of me.

NICO: Why? (Looking up) So I have something on you?

ADONIS: No. (Blushing) Because I feel more beautiful in your gaze.

Sadness

Shape of You | Ed Sheeran

I don't want to *be* sad.
I want to *bed* sadness.

I want to take off her pants,
stretch her underwear to the side,

kiss her between her legs.
She can keep her top on, socks too.

I'd kiss her with all my yearning.
She'd cry, palming her eyes.

I'd kiss her until exhausted, then
I'd lift her from the bed—

                a pool above (pillow)
                a pool below (mattress)—

and carry her to the ocean.
Who am I? I am the squid.

The Cell

moonlight | Dhruv

I pressed my nose to the wall
Nothing will remain of my handsomeness
Your perfume on my pillow and mattress
You shouldn't have come really
I'm afraid of myself because I write
Only an orgasm an invented truth

I'm tired of words that deny my shame
No more jumping in alarm no more consciousness
The walls *Center, Guardian, Refuge, Light of Truth*
I am the end/end-of and also its mercy
People sway and twist in the flames of
The end of the world a wedding song

I'm tearing the ends of my hair
I once said I can do anything
I'm startled by my aloud voice
The world is supernatural in its groveling
I have renewed my affliction
I hear the tick-tock of clocks

There's a full moon tonight
The moonlight is awkward
It stays on the left side of my room
I'm happy there's a defect in my blinds
They don't close so the moon comes in
And the room becomes mouth and tongue

I lie down with eyes open
I idolize my cock in fantastic silence

O masculine
analog of
odorous beauty
animated by
anatomic augmentation
in relation to
and against
imperious muscle
forming a
complete expression
of ephemeral
tautness

Through my window blows a cool breeze
The depth of which is exactly what
My nakedness requires
No more consciousness only an orgasm

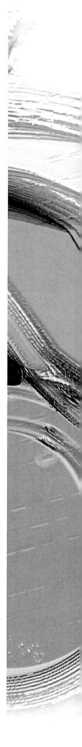

UNION HOTEL

PILLOWTALK | ZAYN

(Thaïs enters the room.)

ADONIS: (Closing the door behind her) The click of a deadbolt to my nervous hands.

GOD: (Offstage) I can see through doors.

ADONIS: (Undressing her) The unbuttoning of a shirt to my astonished heart.

GOD: (Offstage) To me, all souls are naked.

ADONIS: (Undressing himself) The drawing of curtains to my bare silhouette.

GOD: (Offstage) I can see through your nakedness, too.

ADONIS: (Kissing Thaïs' belly) The din of traffic to my absconding lips.

GOD: (Offstage) I can hear a singular voice whispering a hundred feet away in a crowded ballroom.

ADONIS: (Baritone) Now playing, *Union Hotel*, a hotel of parallel universes behind locked doors, adjacent theaters of elopement for God's viewing pleasure.

THAÏS: (Pulling Adonis up) I can't resist your blasphemous announcer voice.

(Adonis and Thaïs embrace. The room recedes into darkness. Sitting in front of this square darkness is God, fluorescent. Quietly, he sits. We look over his shoulder. Who are "we"? A couple of kids who snuck into an adult theater. We do not comprehend what we see. Still, we are filled with excitement.)

THAÏS: (Her forefinger circling Adonis' nipple) It's a moon. (Kissing it) I don't understand your guilt.

ADONIS: I submit to your point of view, Thaïs. Thaïs... When I say your name, my tongue brushes the roof of my mouth.

(They huddle in darkness, naked and immodest.)

THAÏS: I don't understand your guilt. I want to understand it so I can undo it, so I can convince you it's false, a trick. A cell you walk into on your own. I want you like your persona, like when you compose your poems. This is how I want you when you're with me, fumbling with words and syntax and line breaks, talking aloud as you're thinking, not filtering yourself, not censoring yourself, letting your words go, letting your hands go, letting your hands on me.

ADONIS: My hands are candid, I admit. But the rest of my body is a web of guilt. My spine cracks with guilt, my knees creak with guilt, my neck stiffens with guilt, I finish my sentences with guilt, punctuation, self-doubt. There are things I will never write because of my guilt. But you have my hands. They are yours and they are not innocent. They keep secrets. They lock and unlock doors. They remain young while the rest of my body grows old. It's when they are still, they are dishonest.

GOD: (Turning to us) Get out of here!

I am working out the vocabulary of my silence

The Sixth Night: Waking | Muriel Rukeyser

I am working out the vocabulary of my
I am working out the vocabulary of
I am working out the vocabulary
I am working out the
I am working out
I am working
I am
I

=   I hear their unborn voices

Waterfall of The Deepest Place

Baby | Donnie and Joe Emerson

Angels marooned in blue space.
Flying ants born from mist.

A communion of heavy drinking.
Bathers' arms linked from within the waterfall

of the deepest place. Wind from elsewhere?
Or wind of roots?

I can't invent your face and your
mouth newly tattooed.

Fractured spirits climb its tumbling.
They speak an incomprehensible language.

They are born already on the summit,
already gods.

A lantern remained all night.
Unspoken, sacred names in stars' saliva.

ENZO

(Courtyard)

ROACH: (To Adonis) What happened?

(As Adonis recounts his relationship with Enzo, there are cinematic projections of his recollections on a wall.)

ADONIS: (To the roach) I was driving Enzo to the airport.

> Exterior shot: Expressway.
> Interior shot: Front bench seat of car.

ENZO: (Projection) Those are the best filmmakers. They make us reenact a scene. They transform us from spectators into actors.

ADONIS: (To the roach) Then he doesn't say another word, the whole ride. I remember that car well, too. It was a Chevy Lumina, no radio. And terrible brakes. (The roach sighs) When we get to the airport, I park in long-term parking. As we're unloading the bags from the trunk, Enzo says.

> Exterior shot: Airport.
> Interior shot: Parking terminal.

ENZO: (Projection) That's why I blame my divorce on Henry Miller. My suicide on Paul Celan. My purgatory on Tim Burton.

ADONIS: 'They're all men,' I say.

ENZO: (Projection) So?

ADONIS: 'Only one is a filmmaker,' I point out.

ENZO: (Projection) You pay attention to the wrong details. That's why you carry my luggage.

ADONIS: (To the roach) We laughed. (Sighing) Then we go to check in...

ROACH: And?

ADONIS: And I get stopped.

ROACH: What about him?

ADONIS: He gets through. That's the last I saw him.

The Prisoner

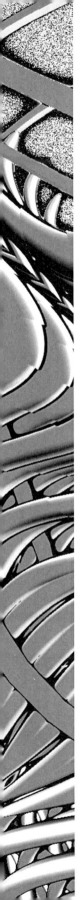

Don't Let Me Be Misunderstood | Nina Simone

The prisoner is a schizophrenic.
The prisoner is sent to Michigan for a test.
The prisoner is accused of falsifying documents.
The prisoner writes on surfaces,
which makes him unpopular with the guards.
The prisoner refuses to eat his meals.
The prisoner feigns indifference but is hypersensitive.

(A brief power outage.)

The bus to Michigan is delayed by a blizzard.
The prisoner is upset because the toilet is broken.
The prisoner has no known family.
The prisoner can pick a lock with a paper clip.

(Another power outage.)

Where is my paper clip?

(The prisoner is putting on a jacket.)

Where is my jacket?

(The prisoner is in the courtyard.)

Fuck! Where is the prisoner?

(The prisoner is being whited out by snow.)

▼ (Desire)

Nannou (EP Version) | Aphex Twin

I've seen all I want to see of my journal:
para-suicide notes next to drawings
of warring UFOs.

> The triangle is the image of my desire,
> the rectangle my coffin, the circle my heart.
> It's a hollow heart.

I've seen all I want to see of my X-rays:
misshapen spine, collapsed hip.
My whole life, forty years,

> and I've gone skinny-dipping only twice.
> Once in Hydra in February, once at night in Montauk
> and I broke my neck.

I've seen, in a broken piece of mirror,
all I want to see of my reflection: bags under my eyes,
crooked nose, cracked lips.

> I look down at my toes.
> These too are crooked.
> Grey water swirls down the drain.

I've seen all I want to see of dawn:
lizards leap across walls, mice rummage
the ceiling. I close my eyes.

> The most unhuman sound swells up.
> A pig being slaughtered.
> All the dust mites and bed bugs gnaw my face.

FUCK YOU

No Silhouette | DPR IAN

(Strawberry Moon)

ADONIS: You're fucked up.

RICHARD: You're fucked up.

ADONIS: You're fucked up.

(Iniquitous guards made plain by diabolic moonlight.)

RICHARD: You fucked up.

ADONIS: You fucked up.

RICHARD: You fucked up.

(The tiniest piece of mirror is always the whole mirror.)

ADONIS: You're fucked.

RICHARD: You're fucked.

ADONIS: You're fucked.

(An entire winter to discover the common roach.)

RICHARD: You fuck.

ADONIS: You fuck.

RICHARD: You fuck.

(I want the words I love you to be just as precise.)

ADONIS: Fuck you.

RICHARD: Fuck you.

Fuck You

Bitter | Meshell Ndegeocello

I want you out of my life.
I don't want to look in the mirror
and see you behind me.
I don't want to hear your voice
in the other room.
I don't want to smell you,
alcohol and smoke on your breath.
I don't want you touching me
to feel your way home.
I don't want to explain why
I feel nothing for you,
a rock I picked up to toss.
I wish you were never born,
not dead—*never born.*

Lorca

Anda Jaleo | Paco de Lucía, Andres Batista, Manolo Sanlucar

He is in the kitchen cooking lentils.
The TV is blaring: Trump won! Trump won!
The neighbors are yelling: Fuck you! Fuck you!
The birds are chirping: War! War!
This is home, he half-says/half-asks.

He goes to a window.
The towers are gone.
The sun and moon switched places.
He puts his palm on the pane.
Night is a wall painted black, he half-says...

He goes to the bathroom.
He splashes water on his face.
Maybe in a different time,
a different war, he half-says...
He looks inside the medicine cabinet.

He walks through the apartment
with his hands gliding
over the walls and furniture.
He picks up a roach.
He places it on the windowsill.

He shuts off the TV.
He retrieves a bowl of lentils.
As soon as he sits down on the couch
there is a hard knocking at the door.
Fuck you! Fuck you! War! War!

MON CHÉRI

Make It Fast, Make It Slow | Rob

NARRATOR: Do you see how it works? The cock speaks.

COCK: (Rising) When you talk
in the sky
I look for

ADONIS: (Roping) Did you ever
a path of
anywhere only not

COCK: (Rising) Ache in such
finery and speech
I see you

ADONIS: (Roping) A little and
a big cry
or it chooses

COCK: (Choking) Dawn at noon
lit air particles
I ride home

ADONIS: (Squeezing) Taut wire field
trilling so many
I don't wanna

COCK: (Pulsing) Whose skipping flared
fuck it I
aye I'm coming

ADONIS: (Quickening) I need it.
                  I need iiiiiiiiirrrrrrggghhh

Moonlight

All Night (Unfinished) | Jai Paul

They are summits
your visits

they reveal to me
direction

not East or West
but inward

to truth—
truths I can

only see or speak
in your company

they are songs
your visits

songs I dance to
even after you leave

My Hotel Room =

Strange Love | Depeche Mode

My own empty beach.

Others arrive by invite only.

I turn up the heat, adjust the lighting.

I pee, wash my hands.

I empty myself, shower.

I stay naked, look at myself in the mirror.

I stretch, breathe deeply into my stomach.

I touch myself... A priming, nothing heavy.

I drink water while I preserve the wine, still corked.

I lay out my gifts on the bed. I wait.

In my waiting, there is a tension.

A pull. A push. A pill.

I go to the window, to the bed, to the window.

My cock swells, bumps into the bed posts.

Then, a jolt—a soft knocking on the door.

I rise up like a wave.

I am, before I even open the door, carried away.

A current. A riptide. An actor in a scene.

There is a suicide. Rebirth. Baptism.

It all plays out in a loop. An hourglass. Infinity...

When I come to,

I see my love recede into architecture and sky.

I linger, unable to move.

Sounds of others' fucking enter the room.

The bits emerge as a faint alarm clock.

I rise, shower, get dressed.

I gather my things, scan the room.

This is my theater.

This is my ocean.

ROOM SERVICE (FOREPLAY)

Under Your Spell | **Desire**

THAÏS: (Opening the door slightly) Hello.

ADONIS: (From hallway, with briefcase) Hello. My name is Mr. Sexy Man. My friends call me, 'Honey Man' or 'Fancy Man.' I work for the hotel. I'm here to offer you a service.

THAÏS: A service? What type of service?

ADONIS: Well, like room service. May I come in to explain further? Here's my ID. (He holds up an ID. It states, 'MR. SEXY MAN' in all caps, and underneath that, 'Employee of the Month.')

THAÏS: Ok, yes. Come in. (She opens the door all the way. Adonis enters the room. She closes the door behind him.)

ADONIS: May I? (He motions to put the briefcase on the bed.)

THAÏS: Yes, you may.

ADONIS: (He places the briefcase on the bed and opens it. He removes several folders overflowing with papers) What I have here are all the services I offer. Plus, some waivers for you to sign, that is, if you select any of the services. I also have in this folder a clean bill of health, (holding up a certificate of sorts) affirming that I'm STD free, (pointing to a date) as of this morning. The hotel mandates that I get tested every day, to retain my services. I don't mind it. It puts me, and the hotel guests, at ease. As for your part, you'll have to sign a document affirming you're also STD-free. I happen to be a notary too. (Thaïs smiles) I will notarize it, free of charge, of course. Once all the legal papers are signed, we can get down to business. (Thaïs burps out a laugh) Oh, I'm sorry! I'm getting ahead of myself. We haven't reviewed the quote-unquote menu, so to speak. I offer everything or anything you want. Oral, vaginal, anal, you name it. But my specialty is eating ass. (Thaïs gasps) Of course, you'll have to clean your ass first. I can tidy up the room while you do. It's what I'd recommend you select. You can pair services too. There's no limit really, except my natural limits, which I've built up to be very impressive, if I say so myself. Oh, may I ask, and please don't be offended, that you confirm you are 21 years old. (Thaïs laughs mischievously) I believe you are, but you have such a youthful appearance, I must confirm by reviewing an official ID. A driver's license will do.

THAÏS: (Smirking) I haven't been carded in ages.

ADONIS: You are, by far, the most exquisite guest I have ever laid eyes upon.

THAÏS: (Mock-revealing an ID) I bet you say that to all the guests.

ADONIS: No, no, not at all! I must confess, quite the opposite. As soon as I saw you check in, I beelined to your room.

THAÏS: Well, I'm glad you did, because I'm expecting company (looking at her watch) in about an hour or so.

ADONIS: Oh. I figured as much. I feel very fortunate then we have this time now, that is, of course, if you select my service. Also, you should know, everything will be billed to your room discretely (winking) as additional cleaning services.

THAÏS: (Laughing) Very sly of you. Well then, in that case, I guess I could pick something. (Mulling over the papers) It's been a while since I've had a thorough ass-cleaning.

ADONIS: (Beaming) There's no time like the present.

THAÏS: Hm. You should know, three men will be coming to my room later, to ravish me. One is my brother-in-law, the other two are football players. They play for the New York Giants.

ADONIS: Whoa! Very impressive! You are full of wonder and surprises. Again, I feel fortunate for the time we have now, before they arrive. But my offer still stands after they come and go. We could postpone the quote-unquote cleaning until then.

THAÏS: No, no. I prefer now. You've persuaded me with your charm.

ADONIS: (Jubilant) Great! Sign here. And here. And here. (Thaïs mock-signs a few papers.)

THAÏS: Let me hop in the shower quickly.

ADONIS: Ok.

THAÏS: (Kissing him) What a spectacle you are.

ADONIS: Do you want me to join you?

THAÏS. No. (Entering the bathroom) I can manage this part alone.

My Own Empty Beach

77 | Kaivon, Kini Solana

I love
an empty
beach. From
the road
it comes
into view
as a horizon
below the horizon.
My own
empty beach!
I undress
and roll
around in
the sand,
offering my
crevices to
its tiny teeth,
its tiny bitemarks.
My own
empty beach!
Look how
it coaxes
me out
of my clothes
into the water.
Look how
the sand
melts away
from my body,
clouding the water.

Anonymous

Cry in the Wind | Clan of Xymox

Not an Adonis, not a player
Not a centaur, not a stud
And not even a ladies' man

Not a smooth operator, not a gigolo
Not a fuckboy, not a swinger
And not even mysterious

Not a pimp, not a hustler
Not a jerk, not a nice guy
And not even an idealist

Not a talkative man, not a life of the party man
Not a popular man, not a comedian
And not even funny

Not an artist, not a writer
Not a musician, not a producer
And not even an indie filmmaker

Not an addict, not an alcoholic
Not a crackhead, not a pothead
And not even a high roller

Not a manager, not a CEO
Not an athlete, not a celebrity
And not even a truck driver

Not a surfer, not a lifeguard
Not a skater, not a baller
And not even a handyman

Not a coach, not a teacher
Not a policeman, not a fireman
And not even a civil servant

You might say not even a man
You might say not even an actor capable of playing a man
You might say not even a man pretending to be an actor capable of
    playing a man

Alone on the couch
Watching a game
On his birthday (or any holiday)

No magazine cover, no published book of poems
No entourage, no ancestors
And not even a citizen

No homeland, no refuge
And not even an asylee

No hero, no prophet
And not even a martyr

No fans chanting his name, no late-night booty calls
No legend, no myth
And not even a good dancer

Not a barfly, not a tough guy
Not an air man, not a mountain man
And not even a fisherman

Not a whispered I love you, not a frantic I love you
Not a bawling I LOVE YOU
And not even a hollered FUCK YOU

Not an immigrant, not a native
Not a local, not a tourist
And not even (nor ever) a host

Not a restauranteur, not a bartender
Not a chef, not a waiter
And not even a busboy

Not an orator, not an interpreter
Not a translator, not an adjudicator
And not even a lawyer

Not a pundit, not an activist
Not a democrat, not a republican
And not even an independent

Not a lewd man, not a politically correct man
Not a fable, not an allegory
And not even a complete sentence

You might say not even a man
You might say not even an actor capable of playing a man
You might say not even a man pretending to be an actor capable of
          playing a man

In Atlantic City
He walks away
From the poker table

(From his wife)
(From his job)
(From his family)

Fully depleted
A hollowed man
Like a defeated boxer

Regaining consciousness in a new world
Not a champion, not a GOAT
And not even a statistic

ADONIS' HEART

FALLING | Che Ecru

(Adonis arrives holding his heart. He holds out his hands to give it to Thaïs.)

ADONIS: Take care of my heart.

THAÏS: How can I?

ADONIS: Take it.

(Thaïs stretches out her hands to receive it.)

THAÏS: I will take, therefore, a light.

ADONIS: To receive a heart can only be done plainly.

THAÏS: Is what remains going to be suffering or pleasure?

(Adonis' heart disappears.)

ADONIS: I shrank. I grew smaller.

THAÏS: Who was I? Who was she?

ADONIS: You were me. She was just a vision. A ghost.

THAÏS: You? No. You were you. Who was I?

ADONIS: You were the eye I passed through, to become me.

THAÏS: And now? That you have passed through.

ADONIS: You are my heart.

THAÏS: No.

ADONIS: You are beautiful.

THAÏS: I am not your beautiful thing.

ADONIS: I know.

THAÏS: What do you see in the mirror? An egress?

ADONIS: I see my name on the marquee. I see a crowd of women who want to marry me.

THAÏS: Ha! A marquee? It's a tombstone, which is to say, a book. And they don't want to marry you, they want to be married, which is to say they want to be carried away. By anyone. They want a parade. Anywhere.

ADONIS: Ouch! What do you see in the mirror? A beach?

THAÏS: I see myself falling. I see a crowd of men that want to fuck me.

ADONIS: That falling is freeness, and it's a gift. Yes, they want to fuck you, but more than that, they want to catch you. They want to play the hero.

THAÏS: And you?

ADONIS: I'm no hero. I'm falling with you. Perhaps a little ahead of you.

THAÏS: Ha, you wish! I'm ahead of you. When I look back, I see you.

(Silhouettes

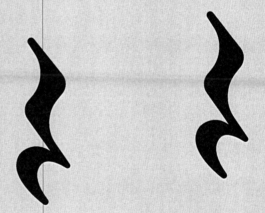

falling)

◐

Become
your
own
myth

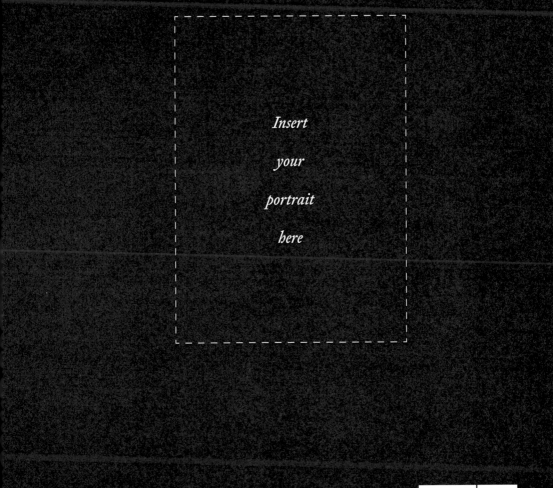

Insert

your

portrait

here

All About U | Rai-Elle

But the beautiful made thing achieves
utility through the illusion of utility—
through sublimity and the illusion it can be
passed through:

—Gregory Pardlo, *"VINCENT'S SHOES"*

I Just Wanna Lay Around All Day In Bed With You | The Coup

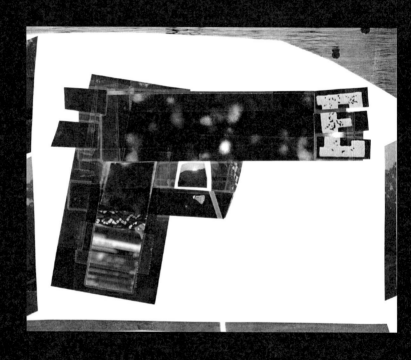

This is a Photograph of Real Life

Just know the grace is not in the landing.
Just showing up is not enough.
When the roach screams "Twelve o'clock!" he voice-activates
the machineries of the curtain.

Intermission. Halftime.
Seventh inning stretch.
The bartender lines up four shots.
Whatever's ahead, it'll be something religious.

In *The Beautiful Made Thing*, Adonis makes Nico into a paramour.
Thaïs directs Adonis' writings,
writings Adonis visits the hospital from.
Nico discovers Adonis' mutation:

two urethras! Two orgasms,
successive, broken by caesura.

Centaur. Liberator of Hearts. Bride of Hell's Kitchen.
The Devil. Characters in a hotel lobby.
Theirs was the love of helium balloons,
the logic of a gun on a wall.

(WEDDING CAKE WITH TOPPER)

MARLEY

Talkin' | **Bob Marley, Dermot Hussey**

(Interview with Bob Marley circa 1974)

MARLEY: So, you can't love my music, if you love reality, you know. You can't love my music like how you would love bar white music. Is different people who love my music from the people who love bar white music. Music never just come in vain, you know.

HUSSEY: That's right. A serious thing.

MARLEY: Music never just come in vain.

HUSSEY: You think the whole question of fame, what it entails, that a part of you belongs to that world of music, you think that's going to change or affect your beliefs in any way?

MARLEY: Can't do that to me, man, you mad. Me in control. You can't change. Anybody change, them did change from long time, man, they no jus' change. They will have that change with them. You understand? Nothing happen, you know. You must understand everything, not a ting happen. Whatever you see, it was there before, man.

HUSSEY: Well, I think people envy you because, this is where they—

MARLEY: They can't envy me, because me hold on upon some, some, me see some big granny a drop and run go save her, and when she let go her weight upon me, me have to make haste to seize her down, and she say "God bless you my son." No, no nobody can take away them blessing from me. Them thing me go through, my friend, you see the lickle friends that you grow with, me no deal with that, you know. Me a come longer than friend. Me was alone by myself long before me meet any friend.

HUSSEY: Hm, hm, I think if people—

MARLEY: I mean, if you can't come up, come, come deal with something right and jus' say to your brethren, "This is what I want to do and make life nice," you figure say, "You must be a hypocrite and start fight." Me start fight because no guy no better than me. People fight me and the more it better for me. Because you see when they fight me, me can go sit down and meditate of what they fighting me for, and make a song of it. How you think me write *I Shot the Sheriff* and all them ting? Just to fight for me a get number one group. You ever shoot at the sheriff?

The Devil

I Shot the Sheriff | Bob Marley

I can see the devil from my window.
He's writing on the sidewalk with chalk.

I can tell from how he moves
he's a dancer, and a fighter.

He's determined too, I can tell
from his eyes looking up, measuring

the approach of several guards.
He's saying something, speaking to the ground,

chant-like. The guards grab his wrists and ankles.
We all lean out of our windows

obscured by fog from our breaths.
He has stopped moving

under weight of knees and shins,
I read his chalked words:

THESE ARE YOUR GODS IF THESE ARE YOUR DOGS I

THESE ARE YOUR GODS

The Two Beasts

I'm Good, I'm Gone | Lykke Li

The Two Beasts are escorting me to HR. They are both leaning into me as we walk side by side, making it difficult for me to not keep stride. The one beast is joking to the other beast how a certain administrator looks like Latoya Jackson. The other beast is laughing heartily. I don't get the joke because I don't see the resemblance, and even if I did see a resemblance, I don't understand how looking like someone else is funny. On this walk to HR, many things are becoming crystal clear to me. 1. I don't get beast humor. 2. These beasts are not my friends. (The beasts don't want to be friends with me either. They do however want everyone else to think we are friends.) 3. These hallways seem a lot narrower now that I am flanked by the two beasts. 4. I need to get out of here! "Here" being my place of work. As for right now though, I am trapped. I have to go through the motions. We arrive at HR. The door is closed, with a sign on it that reads, "We are open. No need to knock. Just come in." The taller beast attempts to open the door, but it's locked. The larger beast knocks on the door. The basic 1-3-2 secret knock. All the administrators use it. Except the taller beast. He's simply an idiot. He genuinely believes all the doors will open for him automatically. And they do, because the other beast opens them for him. The door nudges open. The larger beast paws it wide open and guides me into the office first. I see the back of a small woman walking back to her desk. She hardly acknowledges us entering her office. The two beasts slide in behind me and shut the door behind them. The office feels especially small now with the two beasts and myself inside it. The small woman circles her desk and sits down, facing us. The desk is disheveled with loose papers, sticky notes, two dirty coffee mugs, assorted business cards, thumb drives, a tissue box, a stapler, a scotch tape dispenser, a calculator, a few pill boxes, and a brochure for "Study Abroad." Scotch taped to the walls are pictures of her kids, and grandkids in little league settings and at various graduations. There's an old photocopied sign that reads:

```
COMPLAINT
DEPARTMENT
←
```

The sign is taped to the right of a window. The HR office is on the first floor, so a complaint would survive a fall from here. Underneath that sign, there is a newer photocopied sign that reads:

```
IF IT'S REALLY
FUNNY,
IT'S PROBABLY
HARASSMENT.
```

The taller beast reads the sign aloud, laughs hysterically, then wraps up his laughter with a "That's awesome, dude." An awkward silence precedes the HR woman's "How can I help you?"

THEY WHO ARE MAKING THE FILM

American Money | BØRNS

Exterior: City.

Interior: Industrial loft space.

(God sits at a table, waiting anxiously, clicking his pen. There are a hundred folders on the table. The devil bursts in.)

GOD: Where the hell have you been? You're late!

DEVIL: I missed my train.

GOD: Did you see how many people showed up?

DEVIL: Yes. Did you meet anyone yet?

GOD: No, I was waiting for you.

DEVIL: Good. Are those the headshots?

GOD: Yes.

DEVIL: Ready to start?

GOD: No one's going to do it.

DEVIL: Someone will do it.

GOD: It's wrong for us to ask.

DEVIL: It's genius. Let's go. I'm calling the first person.

(The devil grabs a folder, opens the door and leans out to call a name. The loft is full of waiting actors.)

DEVIL: Adonis? Is there an Adonis?

ADONIS: Yes. Yes! That's me.

DEVIL: Come in. (Closing the door behind Adonis) This is God.

ADONIS: Hello.

GOD: (Remains sitting) Hello.

DEVIL: Do you know why you're here?

ADONIS: Yes, for the lead part.

DEVIL: That's correct.

GOD: Do you know what it is you are auditioning for?

ADONIS: No. Just that it's the lead part.

DEVIL: (Looking through a folder) I see you've done some adult films.

ADONIS: Yes.

DEVIL: God here and I are big fans of the adult industry. All aspiring actors should start there.

ADONIS: I agree.

GOD: (Snatching the folder from the devil) Let's go over the particulars of this part. (The devil and Adonis sit at the table, across from God) The first thing you should know is the project is a multi-year project. If selected, it will require four or five years of your, let's say, service.

ADONIS: No problem.

GOD: Are you married?

ADONIS: Yes.

GOD: Children?

ADONIS: Yes.

GOD: How many?

ADONIS: Two. One girl, one boy.

GOD: How old?

ADONIS: Nine and five.

DEVIL: How about your wife? Is she an actor?

ADONIS: No, no. Far from it. She's a hermit, actually.

GOD: Here's the thing. We're looking for someone with a family.

ADONIS: I'm your man.

GOD: Let me finish. We're looking for someone with a family, like yourself, who would be willing to spend a lot of time, like I said earlier, four or five years at least, away from his family, working on this project.

ADONIS: You mean, on location somewhere?

DEVIL: Kind of.

GOD: Not exactly. You'd be far away from your family.

ADONIS: You mean, I wouldn't be able to see them at all, the whole time we're filming?

GOD: Yes.

ADONIS: Whoa, I don't know...

(A roach crawls out of a folder.)

ROACH: (To Adonis) You go to a dark place, your eyes adjust, your voice changes, you hear things. These things claim you.

(God flicks the roach off the table. The roach lands on its back, on the floor. It rights itself, then calmly disappears under a floorboard.)

GOD: So?

Country

Feelin' Lovely | Connan Mockasin, Devonté Hynes

On the first night, I slept soundly from exhaustion.
My wife seduced me in the morning.

On the second night, I shivered from the cold.
I yearned for the warmth of sunrise.

On the third night, I warred with four mosquitoes.
They remain bloody smears on the wall.

On the fourth night, I dreamt I could fly.
I flew down into a volcano, and hovered there.

On the fifth night, I slept nude and touched myself.
My wife snored loudly beside me.

On the sixth night, a foreign music disturbed my sleep.
What variance there is in music, and insects!

On the seventh night, my hip throbbed with pain.
I had abandoned my cane that morning.

There it is, leaning on the wall, mocking me.
It doesn't throb. It doesn't moan. It's harder than I.

Today

Kiss U Right Now | Duckwrth

I married Thaïs.
I had to marry her. She was dying.

I married her with my track suit and sneakers.
That's when I saw the Stations of the Cross,

elaborate sculptures protruding from gaudy frames.
That's when, standing at the altar,

I saw the cormorant on her shoulder.
Where Thaïs looked, the cormorant looked.

It was thunder-storming outside.
That's when I married Thaïs,

in Hell's Kitchen. My lips pressed her lips
where the cormorant just fed her a shellfish,

a salty pearl, "I do," on her tongue.
And I swallowed her tongue, pearl and all.

ADONIS

(Dive bar)

RICH MAN: (To Enzo) Hello.

ENZO: (Finishing his pint) Hey.

(The bartender sets another pint of stout in front of Enzo, and then acknowledges Rich Man.)

RICH MAN: Scotch. Neat. (Sitting next to Enzo) Have you seen Adonis?

ENZO: (Taking out and lighting a cigarette) He's gone. Disappeared.

(The bartender sets a glass of scotch in front of the rich man. He glances at Enzo's cigarette, but doesn't say anything.)

RICH MAN: I know. I need to find him. Rumor has it he was with you last.

ENZO: (Exhaling smoke) We went to Peyton's. The old triple W. You know it? (Rich Man shakes his head) Nothing special. Not a place you'd go to. (Rich Man sips his scotch) On stage though was the most beautiful woman, with the most amazing body, perfect everything. (Enzo gulps his stout.) Adonis asked her for a lap dance, but so did every other guy, so he had to wait. While he waited, other women solicited him, but he turned them down. He was saving himself for her. (Rich Man sighs.) Finally, when it was his turn, he got so excited... He whispered something in her ear.

RICH MAN: What'd he whisper?

ENZO: I don't know, but whatever he said turned her on, to the 'nth' degree, and she proceeded to give him the best lap dance ever. And I mean the best lap dance ever. (Enzo ashes on the floor.)

But at the end of the dance, she absorbed him into her uterus, and became fully pregnant. For the next nine months she became decreasingly pregnant, until she returned to her original, slim self, with no signs of ever having been pregnant. (Inhaling) Her stage name was Nico The Girl. Her real name was Kelli with an "i."

Vernal Equinox

I know we said no apologies but
I'm sorry I confessed so little
I didn't visit you sooner
Your drifting took you so far
I live in a parallel world
My daring lags behind
I keep sending you letters
Calling them poems
I took so long to get in the Jacuzzi
I insulted language poetry
I didn't turn back—afraid
You wouldn't be looking at me
And that this image would erase all others
I'm sorry

I didn't find your mother's necklace
I still look for it
In thrift stores and flea markets
Do I live in a parallel world?
A fiction of perpetuity?
I overheard someone unwrapping a gift
"No apologies, please"
How could I blame your not-staying?
Then you kiss me through wet hair
And get out before I can kiss you back
Before I smile in this photo you took
I captioned first day in LA
Analogue Adonis
March something 2016

Rivington Street

Motorbike | Leon Bridges

With you comes the sky, the green
of each window, your eyes
looking back at me, a rooftop
of drummers, a city

that keeps getting younger, with so many
lives that separate us, and I—
no longer of this city—I release
all the words that shame me.

I put them in a collage as giftwrap.
You pour two glasses of wine, then step onto
a fire escape. I follow you through
a door held open by a bungee cord.

We're in another country now, on a motorcycle,
no helmets, you're driving, and I can feel the drumming
                through your belly.

PREVIOUSLY THE WEDDING

Touch Me | Victoria Monét, Kehlani

(On the lake)

THAÏS: (To Devil) You may begin.

(Thaïs and Adonis face each other while the Devil recites from the bow of a pontoon boat.)

DEVIL: Adonis, lover of words, seer of inner feelings, compassionate man in a benumbed present, and Thaïs, truthsayer, curator of refurbished hearts, exquisite captain of hanky-panky, have come together here, today, on this dark body of water, before myself and the unrevealed stars above, to formalize their union, and as such will be recognized from this day forward, not as husband and wife, for such terms are reserved for the unimaginative, but rather as comrades in crudity, playmates in slut-hood. With some work still to be done on the honesty side, (to Adonis) yes?

ADONIS: (Solemnly) Yes.

DEVIL: Celebrating the conjoining of two people in this way proclaims openly to all, those who do and do not turn away in their witnessing, today's and tomorrow's witnesses, that these two admire, care, desire, ravish, lust, and yearn for each other's affections. It proclaims the couple's sensitivity to joy and friendship. Yet the ecstasy they experience from their togetherness does not exclude extracurricular pursuits of happiness or new lovers. It proclaims their love as vast and bottomless, as something that cannot be boxed in, to fit other people's dogmas...

THAÏS: No boxes. No dogmas.

DEVIL: They will now say a few words to commemorate this occasion.

THAÏS: (Gazing into Adonis' eyes) The first time you read a poem to me was on the patio of a small café, on Seventh Avenue. We were the only ones there. The night was bright, and humid. Your voice was soft, and shy. It matched your hands. I was trying to be cool, and collected, but my entire being was shaking with forwardness. I had to have you.

(Thaïs kisses Adonis.)

ADONIS: (Gazing into Thaïs' eyes) When you gave me Lorca, you gave me part of yourself, too. I took your hands in my hands. I felt shame, I had nothing to give you. Your hands, I thought, these are hands. I could eat these hands. I could read you a poem. I leaned in, not accidentally, I glimpsed your breasts. The Q train, with the roar of the Cyclone, shattered my reading voice. The sun sunk below the bridge, behind Manhattan. Night fell on us like a blanket. A film played on a wall. The sky, the river, and the ground, all the people, and us, we inched closer in the dark. Our hands... (He grabs her hands) **Our hands broke free in the dark.**

(Adonis kisses her knuckles and sucks on her fingers.)

DEVIL: Yes! I now pronounce you Conjoined Sluts!

(They all strip down and jump into the lake.)

The Lake

Moonage Daydream | David Bowie

Mirror to the night
fireworks, ashtray for shrapnel,
latrine au naturel—blood, wine, piss
on one side, face-washing on the other.

An altar imploding. Dusk
into night, into total darkness.
Such darkness
you're inside it.

Then, slowly, the sun
rises and you can see again
the lake, post-adolescent
in its stillness, its hangover.

Nothing, no blemishes, not even a ripple
from a mosquito's landing,
but underneath the surface, a pulse,
blip, blip, hammering

corpses deeper into the muck,
sending prayers upward
through the gills of fish
into the air of God,

and soldiers drunk on God
toasting the war. *Hoorah.*

I'm Extra Kind to Strangers

Fancy Man | Devendra Banhart

I lend money to my drug-addict friends

I cover for my boss

I go down on prostitutes

When the ATM gives me an extra $20 I return it

I pick up hitchhikers near prisons

I treat my rich friends to dinner

I taxi my neighbors so they don't lose their parking spots

I give directions to my mugger

I tip my bookie on top of the vig

I aid shoplifters and pickpockets

I pray for the Cowboys and Yankees

I call my arresting officer sir

I stick up for the meter maid

I vouch for liars and cheats

I warehouse contraband for free

I flush all the urinals in public restrooms

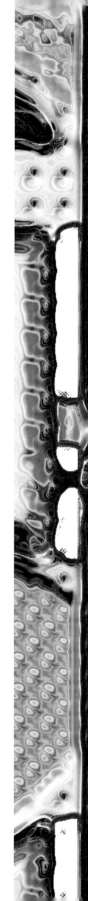

THE BEAUTIFUL MADE THING

Licking an Orchid | Yves Tumor, James K

(*Untitled* at The Whitney)

ADONIS: In the shadow of the beautiful made thing is the one who is betrayed, the one who suffers the greatest loss. The loss of a lover, or a child. The one who is left behind, and stays behind.

NICO: The one who does not change.

ADONIS: The one who does not change. (Adonis dozes off)

(Adonis awakens)

ADONIS: The beautiful made thing does not rest. It's always in flight. Take, for instance, a total solar eclipse. Decades of travel predate its arrival, and follow its departure. One does not intercept, or possess it. One witnesses, or experiences it.

NICO: One is wounded by it.

ADONIS: One is wounded by it. (Adonis loses consciousness)

(Adonis regains consciousness)

ADONIS: Games are the offspring of the beautiful made thing. Imagine an epic game of hot potato. One catches and tosses the steaming globe in one fluid motion. If one holds it too long...

NICO: She burns her hands.

ADONIS: She burns her hands. The required rhythm reflects the perfection of the beautiful made thing. The drop signifies its fragility.

NICO: Perfection's impermanence.

ADONIS: Those who recognize it. And those who don't. (Adonis dies)

(Adonis is reborn)

ADONIS: What if I am...

NICO: A glare. What does it mean to be a glare?

Beacon

Beautiful Escape | Tom Misch, Zak Abel

So, after you left, I felt like I was in a spaceship, in the pilot's quarters, hurling through space at 10,000 miles per hour. The window, or windshield, was framed in an X, and a red light or a red haze constantly hugged it. Naturally, I assumed, this red light is from the heat of the spaceship cutting through the freezing cold atmosphere of space. It heated the room, and I felt warmer because of it. I also felt myself moving, flying, and so remained half-awake, in and out of sleep, through the night. I was alone, yes. But I was on a journey born from you, from us, our meeting. I felt that you launched me in this spaceship, by hitting some secret eject button that flung me, with minimal information and instruction. I would have to figure it out. I trusted your coordinates. Then, another possibility entered my mind: we began this journey together, it was our journey. But something was pulling you back, you couldn't leave earth, there were loved ones that needed saving, or if not saving, they needed comforting. You couldn't leave them. So you found an escape pod, said something to me through the pod which was inaudible, and returned to earth. You said: Adonis, you got this. Or was it: My ukulele, bring back my ukulele. I traveled the cosmos in a few hours bathing in your afterglow. Your smell filled my nose and mouth and lungs, and covered me like a sheet, not a blanket, its warmth tickling me just enough to keep me awake. It felt more like I was floating than lying down. I was floating on a bed that was floating, and floating so near to it, on top of it, I would brush it, gently, tenderly. I felt whole, and three-dimensional, and for this reason, even though I was alone, I did not feel alone. I felt like a nucleus, and my limbs, the outer parts of my body, were simply invisible. My limbs were all the other people, the stars, all the other planets, everything. It was incredible, and timeless, but fleeting, I could sense it. Then, gradually, without the possibility of ever noticing or naming the exact moment, the red light dissipated and was replaced by a diffuse, flat light. It was the light of morning in any city, USA. It signaled an arrival, and a loss. I was no longer in a spaceship. I wasn't moving or floating. I was heavy, pressed down into the bed by a giant invisible hand. I felt two-dimensional. I was an ant on a sidewalk, or a windowsill. I was vulnerable. I was a bull's eye to any obnoxious child. But then, getting up, I found your portrait. I was looking at myself sort of smiling back at me. And I sort of smiled at the portrait, trying to be its reflection. The two of us with the sort of smile you gave us. This was our outside voice. This was us guarded, uncertain. But, on the inside, I swelled up with a new happiness, a new sense of hope and wonder and excitement. Because you saw me and remade me, and in this way, you were still seeing me and showing me myself. And I could hear my inside voice say: You got this!

Love Poem for My Love

Love U Better | Victoria Monét

I masturbate with a new intent
to make myself a better lover for you

I penetrate myself
so I may feel what you feel

I touch myself
so I can measure the weight of my touch

I taste myself
so I may sweeten myself for you

I exercise
so when I'm with you I last

I make playlists
so we have a guide for our lovemaking

so after you leave I have a soundtrack
to masturbate to

I deny myself certain pleasures (a chocolate croissant)
so I come to you hungry (manic)

I drive my car (to pick you up and drop you off)
so I become a vehicle for your pleasure

I make myself sore
so I know pain from your absence

I brush my teeth
so when I eat your pussy you feel a minty tingle

I empty myself
so you may fill me up

I lotion my hands
so I may rub your feet

I go shopping
so I can dress you up to undress you

I gather gifts
so I never arrive empty-handed

I manicure my fingernails
so as not to scratch you

I practice yoga
so I may hold myself up

so I can climb on top of you
and not crush you with my weight

I clean myself
so I may be a spring for you

I contort myself
so I may learn the limits of your flexibility

I seek a rhythm
finding and losing it

so I may find my way back to it instinctively
so I will not lose you more than briefly

OPEN MIC' NIGHT

We Should Be Together | **Pia Mia**

GOD: (On stage) I am the shame stuck in your throat. Open your mouth and turn loose mourning. I am acid rain filling your reservoirs. Drink me and your thirst multiplies. I am the prisoner on Death Row. The face of anyone who looks in a mirror. I am the fetus wrapped in explosives. All around me, light; all around the light, darkness. I am the heart taken from the chest of one man and put in the chest of another. At first, I stutter, then, I find my rhythm.

DEVIL: (Solo standing applause) Bravo! Bravo!

(Later that night at a dive bar.)

GOD: (Drawling) Bow down to the beer. Bow down to the beer. Bow down to the beer. Bow down to the beer…

DEVIL: (To Bartender) Another round over here.

GOD: (To Devil) I miss you, man. I miss us. (Burp) I miss us hanging out.

DEVIL: We're hanging out now.

GOD: This doesn't count. (Looks around) This place is a hospice for drunks.

DEVIL: I know. It's perfect.

(The bartender places two fresh pints in front of them.)

GOD: (Gulping) It's perfect for drunks. Not for us. You and me… We should go to… Wo Hop!

DEVIL: (Gulping) I could go for some baby clams in black bean sauce.

GOD: That's what I'm talking about! Let's go.

DEVIL: I'll drive. (They down their beers)

GOD: (Standing up) Die Gnade Morphium, aber nicht die Gnade eines Briefs, die Gnade Menschen, Worte, Sprüche, aber nur im Delirium die einzige Erscheinung, auf die alles wartet.

(God turns his pockets inside out, revealing nothing but a crumpled paper, which he throws on the bar.)

DEVIL: (To Bartender) For the drunk, there can be only one torture, that which is not drunkenness. (He puts a $100 bill on the bar) To experience the world sober is a crucifixion.

(They exit. The bartender puts the bill in his pocket, uncrumples the piece of paper:

> I drowned a moth in my pee
> I thought it'd be more buoyant
> I eulogized the moth as Enzo
> I made the sign of the cross
> I bowed my head in silence
> I shook out the last trickles
> Then Enzo flew up
> & grazed my head
> Bravo Enzo!
> Bravo!

He recrumples it, and tosses it in the garbage. But he remembers it a little later, at the urinal, when he pisses on a fly.)

Peyton's Play Pen

disco tits | Tove Lo

Λ poacher's station
its surplus of gruesome specters
a tavern of hoary expatriates

I enter, a hesitant intruder
unfolding skins in moonlight
searching for blemishes with charred fingertips

where I expected a tomb
I find an apparatus for anesthesia
I construct a filthy ocean—and I drink from this

The Girlfriend Experience

Fuckboy | BAUM

A man has three impulses:
the cock, the heart, the brain—
in that order!

The cock's impulses are animalistic.
The heart is under constant attack (a deluge of lies!)

so it can't recognize love.

The brain is lure and lawyer.
As lure, it snares what the cock desires.
As lawyer, it defends the cock's actions

and rationalizes them for future litigation.
It's when the brain deceives the heart
that a man feels like a God.

This is when he anoints himself an Adonis.
This is when he comes to me,
and I feed him his delusions, in spades.

But before I feed him,
I sit on his face. Forget GFE.
It's all about "Queening."

THE COURTYARD

I'll Be There For You/You're All I Need | Method Man, Mary J. Blige

(Adonis is resting his back against a wall. The roach is on his lap. They are sharing a joint.)

ROACH: Did you ever deal?

ADONIS: No, never. But Enzo did. When we lived together in college. Though, he wasn't any good at it.

ROACH: How so?

ADONIS: He smoked more than he sold. And he gave the rest away, you know, at parties and stuff. Plus, he had so much of it. Too much, really. The stuff was everywhere. I'd open my closet and find garbage bags full of it. All my clothes reeked.

ROACH: Why'd you help him?

ADONIS: I owed him.

ROACH: What'd you owe him?

ADONIS: I don't know. I felt like I owed him. So, when he asked me to help him collect some money from some deadbeat, I agreed. Then he stuffed his .22 in his pants and handed me an air rifle. An air rifle! Can you believe that? Before I understood what was going on, I was standing in a strange apartment in Detroit, and Enzo had his .22 in this guy's back, forcing him to search for money. I remember feeling way out of my league. I mean, yeah, we were high and all, but that doesn't explain it. I mean, the way he controlled this guy, the way he moved him through the apartment, it was cartoon-like. It was as if he reached into his back and was steering him from a control panel, or joystick, or something.

ROACH: That was some stuff you were smoking!

ADONIS: Ha! Yeah, I guess.

ROACH: Did you get the money back?

ADONIS: No. Of course not! There was no money. We grabbed a bunch of CDs and trinkets, and split.

ROACH: Then what?

ADONIS: I don't remember. I don't remember the rest of that night. Or much else from that time. I heard, later on, Enzo quit selling and disappeared. Maybe to Hawaii. I'm not sure where he went, or what he's up to. Or if he's even alive. But I still have the CDs.

ROACH: The CDs?

ADONIS: Yeah, Prince's Purple Rain, Lee Perry Meets The Mad Professor, Wu-Tang...

Outside

Childish Gambino | Feels Like Summer

The world is open, mocking
my poverty, my confinement.

The world stands guard
against me—a little, wicked guard!

The world fits miserably
in the frame of my window.

The world is a blue wall of silence,
afraid to speak its own thoughts.

I see seagulls pregnant with hunger
rummaging the jetties, policing the tide—

little, wicked guards cutting the air like Chinese stars.
I make a gun from my index finger and thumb.

I point and shoot. I point and shoot,
clicking my tongue. Click. Click-click-click.

(Evergreen) Forest

Something Just Like This | The Chainsmokers, Coldplay

So we might be together,

parts of us (that barely belong to us—

we inherited them) will have to be sacrificed,

leaving us with our art.

A secret life

with diary will be our honeymoon suite.

Once I slept in a forest,

in the rain, under a fir tree,

wet and wrinkled as a squid, and I was happy.

I feel most alive when I'm with you.

For us, that means anime

and helium heart balloons and pillow talk, to liberate fully.

The lost balloons (up they go) do not bother me.

I'm with you. In the clouds, and ocean.

THAÏS

Jaguar | **Victoria Monét**

(Hospital)

THAÏS: Guess who came to see me today?

NURSE: No idea, tell me.

THAÏS: Adonis, my dear.

NURSE: And who, might I ask, is Adonis?

THAÏS: (Handing her a photograph) My Borges.

NURSE: Oh. (Winking) Handsome.

THAÏS: He brought me oysters.

GOD: (Massaging Thaïs' feet) What a succulent lunch.

NURSE: Aren't you allergic?

THAÏS: Yes. But it's the thought that counts.

GOD: It's better to love than be loved. That's what I always say.

NURSE: (To God) You're no more comforting than a sheet.

GOD: (Kneeling) No one asked you. (Retrieving a necklace from under the bed) Thaïs, do you have a necklace with the evil eye?

NURSE: What a beautiful necklace!

THAÏS: It's an omen.

GOD: (Getting up) It must be from the previous patient. A Greek woman who caressed my face.

NURSE: (To God) What is it you do here?

GOD: Float. Like a jellyfish. Because it's better to be a jellyfish... Than an oyster!

THAÏS: Ha! Owe! Ooh, it hurts when I laugh.

NURSE: Where was this taken?

THAÏS: Paris, in May. A gift for my fortieth birthday... We were walking along the Seine... His eyes were yellow, and then they were green, and then they were brown. In a matter of a sunset. As soon as it was dark, he became frisky. Yes, he would flirt in the daytime too. But in the night, in the night he was all hands. He would hook my arm, or circle my waist. He'd tuck a strand of hair behind my ear. Then he'd tickle my earlobes to admire my earrings. He'd take off my wedding band, put it on his pinkie finger, wear it for a few minutes and then return it to a different finger. There was a formula to his seduction, I learned. Little by little, and then more and more, his hands would brush my stomach, my chest, my ass. Suddenly, his hands would be under my blouse. And we'd still be in public. Ah, in these moments, I'd want to race back to the hotel. But he'd want to stay out...

(Two children run into the room.)

CHILDREN: Mama. Mama.

CHILD 1: (He takes out a plastic gun and shoots God.) Bang! You're dead. (God falls to the ground.)

(The child points the gun at the nurse. She puts her hands up.)

CHILD 2: Cockle-doodle-doo! I'm a rooster.

(God crawls out of the room.)

THAÏS: My children! I missed you so much! (She scoops them up into bed with her. She hugs them firmly.)

(A businessman and a lady in a fine hat appear in the doorway.)

BUSINESSMAN: Are you afraid?

THAÏS: I'm escaping.

BUSINESSMAN: From what?

THAÏS: From you, and your mother.

BUSINESSMAN: What do you want?

THAÏS: There is this heaviness in my chest. It's as if my heart is too heavy for my body.

BUSINESSMAN: (Annoyed) And?

THAÏS: So, I want to be an enormous beast. A giant known for the heaviness of its organs. With the stamina to carry them around effortlessly. But I cannot. Because... Where would I put my fishnet stockings? Where my tequila and cigarettes? What a horrible life, a life without secrets...

BUSINESSMAN: You can keep your secrets. I'll take the children back.

THAÏS: Goodbye children. (She kisses them.)

CHILDREN: Mama. Mama.

(The lady in a fine hat gathers the children and they all leave holding hands.)

NURSE: (To audience) They drag her children away as if walking dogs. Two brutes with pockets full of gauze. They dare not look in the rooms they pass. As for the children... Two cherubs who struggle to keep up with their masters. They look into the rooms and see their fear of being left behind.

THAÏS: (To audience) Memories immense and sad like those of a horrible labor, a child's name erased, a biking accident, a camping trip... Deep well memories. Memories of a naïve girl. Terribly clumsy. Terribly brave. Memories of a volcano...

(They look out the window. There is a low, yellow moon, just above the skyline.)

THAÏS: Full moon tonight.

NURSE: The werewolves are out.

(Enter Adonis.)

NURSE: Visiting hours are over.

THAÏS: He can stay.

(The nurse exits. Adonis climbs into bed with Thaïs. They spoon.)

THAÏS: I have K-Y jelly in the drawer.

ADONIS: Later.

(They both sigh. One from self-pity, the other relief. Then, recognizing each's innermost feelings, they sigh again.)

THAÏS: (In a low voice) I don't want to keep taking my medicine.

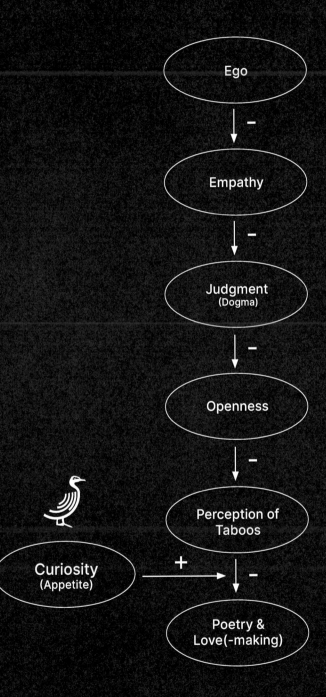

Ego

│ −
▼

Empathy

│ −
▼

Judgment
(Dogma)

│ −
▼

Openness

│ −
▼

Perception of
Taboos

Curiosity
(Appetite) ──── + ────▶ │ −
▼

Poetry &
Love(-making)

Huit october 1971 │ Cortex

Interminably the Apogee

Tell Me | Neil Frances, The Undercover Dream Lovers

This is the book of those who yearn deeply,
who speak one way on the page, and another off it:

This is the beautiful made thing of those who make things,
for whatever occasion, who make things they let go:

This is the audience, in the third act, in the arc of Adonis'
life, where his exhaustion eclipses his burning:

This is the tenderness of those making playlists,
skimming lyrics, the salty taste of words:

     us, swimming in the ocean.

Los Angeles

We called it OBLIVION barely knowing ITS GRAVITY
I weighed each word on my tongue before speaking

We called it TEN YEARS barely knowing THIS MOMENT
I didn't want to overwhelm you as overwhelmed as I was

We called it SPATIAL POETICS barely knowing TEXTURE
I held your phone and iterated directions

We called it KARMA barely knowing JEALOUSY
I understood we carried an audience in our pockets

We called it GREEKTOWN barely knowing THE LYRICS
I drank continuously nodding my head

We called it FUCKING barely knowing OUR APLOMB
I unburied you from comforter and pillows

We called it NO FEAR barely knowing HOW IT WOULD FEEL
I stayed awake all night listening to your breathing

We called it MOST QUOTED barely knowing KEATS
I preserved discord of title and cover art

We called it TURBULENCE barely knowing HOLLOWS OF SKY
I felt myself in freefall in acquittance

We called it ORGANIC barely knowing SEEDS OF THINGS
I found your necklace with evil eye broken

We called it NARRATIVE barely knowing OUR CANCERS
I wrote our story backwards

We called it TOTEM hoping IT WOULD HAVE SOUL
I glued the pieces back together

                                        hoping IT WOULD REDEEM US
The pieces however did not fit perfectly

ADONIS GIVES A READING (& BOOK SIGNING)

I Want You | Erykah Badu

ADONIS: (On stage)…A quatrain, in tribute to Omar Khayyám, titled,

Not Exactly A Translation, But Still.

I sip a cup of coffee as if kissing.
I half-taste, half-anticipate its essence, the divinity,
asking of it, its secrets. Then, interrupted,
it replies by scolding my tongue! Still, I sip on.

(Adonis signs books after the reading. First in line is the Devil.)

ADONIS: I owe this book to you.

DEVIL: You owe me nothing.

(Adonis inscribes: You have given me everything,
including your life, multiple times.
You have been a brother, and a father
to me. You taught me honesty begins with deceit,
happiness with sadness, art with ugliness,
and friendship without expectations.
Integrity is not a mode,
it's in how you fuck.)

DEVIL: You are my star pupil. God is so jealous.

(Second in line is God.)

GOD: Of me, you ask the impossible.

ADONIS: Ours was the love of those who take pleasure in denying.

(Adonis inscribes: 'Like suicides, gods change with men.' —Camus)

GOD: (Huffing) No sir.

(Third in line is Nico.)

ADONIS: I'm so glad you came.

NICO: I wouldn't miss it.

(Adonis inscribes: I can't drink Malbec anymore,

                          or listen to Coltrane, without thinking of you.

                          I see you standing in every window,

                          a city behind you, a rainy night.

                          I look for you in indie bookstores and film theaters,

                          and I find you! in the inexpressive.

                          I love how when you smile demonically,

                          you bite your lower lip, like Molly Ringwald.

                          I wish for you to be an alien,

                          so you can abduct me and take me

                          to your faraway planet.

                          This will save me so many painful goodbyes.

                          I love how when I look at you looking at me,

                          I see myself, as someone else,

                          someone new, someone I could still become.

                          —Did you know 'scène' in French also means 'stage'?)

ADONIS: Thank you.

NICO: I got to run. (They kiss on both cheeks.)

(Fourth in line is Roach.)

ROACH: You're still alive.

ADONIS: You too, I see.

(Adonis inscribes: Beware the heel, with a face like yours.)

ROACH: Beware the evil eye, when you look over your shoulder.

(Fifth in line is Rich Man.)

RICH MAN: I found you!

ADONIS: Ah me.

RICH MAN: There's a large debt I wish to collect.

ADONIS: I don't subscribe to your economics.

(Adonis inscribes: You can appeal anything. Such is your entitlement. But that's not the same as getting whatever you want, whenever you want it. Your delusion is a cowbell.)

RICH MAN: Oh, I will collect.

(Sixth in line is RICHARD.)

RICHARD: Adonis.

ADONIS: Richard.

(Adonis inscribes: Fuck you.)

RICHARD: Fuck you! (He storms off, with his signed book.)

(Seventh in line is Ellen.)

ELLEN: Are we good?

ADONIS: No.

(Adonis inscribes: The loneliest person in the world is surrounded by "friends" at work.)

ELLEN: How could you?! (Ellen storms off, crying.)

(Eighth in line is Enzo.)

ENZO: Kilroy!

ADONIS: Greedo!

ENZO: I brought you a gift. (He passes him a joint.)

ADONIS: Thanks, man. (They embrace.)

(Adonis inscribes: You are yourself, always.

                       If I invent your presence, it's because

                       I'm constantly getting lost in my solitude.)

(Ninth in line is Thaïs.)

THAÏS: My Borges.

ADONIS: My Thaïs. (They embrace.)

THAÏS: Would you be so kind?

ADONIS: Of course. Or, I could later, no?

THAÏS: I prefer now.

ADONIS: Ok.

(Adonis inscribes: In my first book, you were you,

                       that is, you were the you of all my love poems.

                       In my second book—here I plead for mercy

                       and understanding—I have merged you,

                       I have obscured you, I have disfigured you

                       by combining your features, our memories,

                       with the features and memories of others.

Please, steel yourself against any perceived blemishes,
any jealousy. And know that when I close my eyes
at night, tonight, it's you, always you, I move towards.)

Adonis' Cock

Pony | Ginuwine

Who will lift it in their hands?
Who will smash it with a hammer?

Adonis goes out with a stiff cock
Interfering with his gait, making his butt stick out
And occasionally he has to stop, and stand still
Perform the slightest wiggle in his hips

It's nearly noon
The bus is crowded with beachgoers

Inside the cock is the sound of water
Adonis murmurs:
Can you see any light?
Can you see your mother?

The cock sighs: A dozen lovers!
Adonis (blushing) smiles at Thaïs

Thaïs lifts Adonis' cock in her hands
Studies it, places it on her blanket
What happened to the foreskin?
Cut off at birth

Inside the cock is the sound of water
A stadium chanting

Slowly summer was ending with a shower
Having intercourse with Thaïs

COMPLAINT DEPARTMENT

The Piano Has Been Drinking (Not Me) | **Tom Waits**

(HR office)

ELLEN: For me, trust is everything. I need to trust the people I work with. I understand not everyone is a sharer. That is, they don't share what they do on their personal time, over the weekend, etcetera, with me or their colleagues. I get it. Some people are very quiet and very private. But I'm a sharer, and I need to know, really know, the people I'm working with, otherwise I can't trust them. (Looking at Adonis) I need to know things like, are you married, who are your friends, what are your politics, do you support veterans, do you put your hand over your chest for the pledge of allegiance, or do you take a knee? Do you use drugs?

RICHARD: I smoke weed. Not every day, not at work. But at shows, and at practice. I'm in a band. (He motions with his hands as if he's playing the drums.) Drummer.

ELLEN: Things like, are you an alcoholic? So I can help you. Are you happy at work? Do you like the people you work with? Are you having marital problems? Going through a divorce? (Ellen and Richard glance at each other) Or, are you a cheater?

RICHARD: A womanizer.

ELLEN: There is counseling for these things. One, I care about the well-being of my workers. Two, these are things I need to know so I can work with you, so I can trust you.

HR WOMAN: Actually, you don't need to know any of those things. It's highly improper for you to ask those things in my presence.

ELLEN: I don't think so.

RICHARD: We don't think so.

ELLEN: Well, I don't need answers to those specific questions right now, this minute, but (looking at Adonis) I need to know I can trust you. However you can prove to me I can trust you, that's what's important to me. I know I can trust my friends, because I know them, I know who they are, I know who they are married to. I know Richard is married to Zena, and that Zena's an amazing woman.

RICHARD: Zena's great. I'd be lost without her.

ELLEN: I know I can trust him because Zena chose him as her husband. That's what I'm talking about.

ADONIS: Would you like to meet my wife? I could give you her resume.

HR WOMAN: No! We are not asking that. Ellen is just speaking figuratively.

RICHARD: Does your wife know you are cheating on her?

HR WOMAN: Richard!

RICHARD: What? He is. We have witnesses.

ELLEN: (To Adonis) I just don't trust you anymore. (To HR Woman) I'd like to write him up.

HR WOMAN: So, write him up.

ELLEN: I'd like to say what I want to write him up for, and you write him up.

HR WOMAN: (Sighing) Ok, what would you like to write him up for?

ELLEN: For being aloof, and (glancing at Richard) for not treating Richard with more respect.

RICHARD: He looks at me with disdain.

HR WOMAN: (Shuffling through some papers) Here we go. His annual evaluations from the last eight years. (Skimming them) These seem to be very, very positive. I don't understand. I am not sure what's going on here.

(Richard lunges at the desk, grabs all the papers from the HR Woman's hands, and jumps through the window, breaking the glass. He lands on his hind legs and runs into the street, weaving through moving cars until he disappears around a corner. Ellen roars. Loose papers fly up and out the broken window. Adonis and the woman hide behind the desk. In one motion, Ellen lifts the desk and consumes it. She then consumes the HR woman. Adonis leaps out the window and runs in the opposite direction of Richard. Ellen roars out the window, regurgitating the HR woman, who falls on the sidewalk, seemingly ok.)

Sun & Moon

I'm tired of lying.

I want to say something meaningful.

We are silhouettes, more than shadows of our words.

I have no faithfulness.

But I have made speeches in empty hotel rooms.

I have burrowed my face lovingly in an asshole.

The road I have followed is strewn with forks

       and side trails into overgrown brush.

Forgive me.

What is base in this book is mine.

All mine.

I'll tell you what turns me on.

The sexiest thing of all is your breasts and armpits

       with your arms above your head.

Sun and moon, lake and stars.

I have lived because I have loved, *and* I have fucked.

Is there any greater oeuvre?

That is the secret to immortality.

I resent not my aging but the aging of my lovers.

Sex is my God *and* my Devil.

God v. Devil

Soul Control | Jessie Ware

Game 1

He breaks. No balls go down. He says, 'That was God. This is the Devil.' He knocks down a striped ball. 'The Devil is stripes.' He sips his beer in-between turns. He's not very good as God, or as the Devil. He finishes the first beer, opens another one. God makes a hell of a shot! He hoots and hollers. The Devil smirks, then follows with a banker that makes God gasp. After matching impressive shots, they go back and forth with some awful play. A disco song comes on. It's God's playlist. He starts dancing around the table, nicely buzzed. He loses track of whose turn it is. God goes. He sinks a nice long shot. The Devil knocks in two in a row. God misses a hanger. The Devil makes his next shot, and is left with just the 8-ball. He takes a deep breath, stills his hips, aims, and shoots. Devil 1, God nil.

Game 2

God wants a rematch. This time the Devil breaks. Nothing. God knocks down a striped ball. 'God is stripes.' More awful play. Minutes tick by. God scratches. The Devil knocks down two. God knocks down two. The Devil one. God one. The Devil makes a behind the back shot. He smiles. God shrugs his shoulders. The Devil misses. Then, God makes the shot of the night—an acute angle, with the perfect weight on the shot. He knocks in two more. The Devil has one rattle in and out. God lines up the 8-ball for the win. He misses. The Devil misses. Now, God is facing a hanger. He opens another beer, dances around the table, rubs extra chalk on the cue stick. 'Oh life,' he says, then shoots. Devil 1, God 1.

Game 3 (The Rubber Match)

The Devil racks. God breaks. Nothing. The Devil knocks down a striped ball. It's not lost on either of them, stripes keeps winning. The Devil knocks in two more, to make it three in a row. More awful play. The Devil nearly knocks in the 8-ball prematurely. God knocks in a couple, then scratches. The Devil positions the cue ball favorably. He knocks in that shot, and then one more. He only has two balls left to God's five. God knocks in one. The Devil knocks in one. It's one to four now. God makes a nice shot, then follows up with a miss. The Devil makes a banker, but he leaves himself in terrible position for the 8-ball. All three of God's remaining balls block his line. Still, he manages to hit the 8-ball, but it doesn't go in.

Instead, he knocks in one of God's balls. God misses. The Devil announces, 'Side pocket. If I make this, we're going to Play Pen.'

ASTRONAUT

One And Four (AKA Mr.Day) | John Coltrane

(Church)

PARISHIONERS: What the... (Incoherent mumbling)

(The parishioners are bewildered by a series of new paintings that have replaced the Stations of the Cross. They gather around them to read their captions. In disorganized groups, they move from one caption to the next, talking irritably. This goes on for a bit, then an astronaut emerges from the altar.)

ASTRONAUT: I want this. (He holds a photo up to the audience.) The parallel universe alternator. (The parishioners squint.) I found it in an attic in New Jersey. I thought it was an old tape recorder, but it has no slot to insert a tape of any kind. (He turns the photo inward to himself.) It has several buttons with no labeling, or any variance in color. (He lowers the photo.) When I cleaned it up and placed it on my kitchen table, it looked like the base of a high-voltage blender. As I was looking it over, studying it, I experienced this strange sensation that it was returning my gaze with equal suspicion. Frightened, I exclaimed aloud, 'What the fuck?!' It immediately muttered something. I said it again. Again, it emitted an obscure reply. I pressed one of the buttons, leaned in, and offered a clear, unmuffled 'What the fuck?!' This time it spit out something more audible. It sounded like three people cursing at the same time: 'Fuck-off!' 'Fuck-you!' and 'Fuck-face!' (He raises the photo.) I asked 'What God is this?' This time it spat out: 'God almighty!' 'Allah the merciful!' 'The Buddha within!' all spoken at once with 'ful' standing out at the end. (He lowers the photo.) I thought it best to keep quiet for a while, and not make any utterance. Cautiously, I grabbed a pen and paper, and began writing a scene. At first, I began writing a scene from my life. Then that lead to a new scene, an original scene. (The parishioners stir.) I then read the scene aloud, pausing after each sentence to hear the machine translate my sentence. Each sentence it translated was eerily similar, but dissimilar too, to mine. Often times, it offered a more dramatic, poetic sentence. I was getting pretty excited.

With this machine, I strategized, I could write one scene and get three additional scenes, for a total of four scenes. Why stop with scenes? I could write a full screenplay, and get three additional screenplays! At first, I thought, I have to keep this prolific machine hidden from my peers. But now, I believe, it must be a key of some kind. It could be the key to world peace. It could be the key to everlasting happiness. Or it could be the key to unlocking time travel—

PARISHIONERS: Or it could be the key to the apocalypse!

ASTRONAUT: (Pondering) Or it could be the key to the apocalypse, yes. That's possible, that is, if one thinks the apocalypse is still ahead of us, and not behind us.

PARISHIONERS: What devil is this that speaks from the pulpit?!

ASTRONAUT: (Removing his helmet) ...

Birthday Suit | Kesha

1. Thaïs is diagnosed with cancer.

2. Thaïs is placed inside a machine.

3. Thaïs becomes the infected nucleus.

4. Thaïs greets her visitors with a mechanical voice.

5. Adonis reads to Thaïs, Lorca's *Fable and Round of the Three Friends*.

6. The Devil kisses Thaïs' on her belly.

7. Thaïs stirs from the gesture.

Stations of Thaïs

14. Thaïs escapes into Hell's Kitchen.

13. Thaïs dresses in a gown (no bra, no underwear).

12. Thaïs grabs her breasts.

11. Thaïs is resuscitated.

10. Thaïs is removed from the machine.

9. Thaïs faints from dehydration.

8. Thaïs dismisses Adonis and the Devil.

143

Oscar Wilde

In Oscar Wilde there is a urinal
with the letters *L I A R* as a face
For this reason
in a city of however many million people
I no longer feel safe
I no longer trust anyone

Because Oscar Wilde knew
I was coming here before I knew it
Oscar Wilde knew
how my life would turn out
before I knew
and then engraved it
in porcelain
as epitaph
in a basement bathroom

I'm pissing on my grave
before I lie in it
while everyone upstairs is laughing and toasting
and immortal
including Thaïs who is waiting for me
to take her to Paris

144

DEVIL'S PRAYER

Come Over | Ce'Cile, ZJ Chrome

(Adonis is lying in bed looking up at the ceiling.)

DEVIL: (Offstage) Come on, Adonis, come over. Come and look, Adonis. The world is so angry, and about to explode. Come and see, Adonis. The world fears our existence. Come and listen, Adonis. The world booms with ice cracking. Come, Adonis, and hear—what the world sounds like underwater.

(Adonis gets up and goes into the bathroom. He splashes water on his face and looks in the mirror.)

DEVIL: (Offstage) Come and feel, Adonis. The face of the world is coarse. Come and touch, Adonis. The lips are cracked with sun poisoning. Come and smell, Adonis. The world began with a fart. A cosmic fart. Come on, Adonis, come for the aroma. Being the world is the punishment.

(Adonis removes his clothes and gets into the shower.)

DEVIL: (Offstage) Adonis, come and I will cook for you, my curry. And, Adonis, if you can handle it, my vindaloo. You can gobble it up.

(Adonis tilts his head back and gurgles the water as it comes out of the showerhead.)

Coney Island

Mr. Sexy Man | Nellie Tiger Travis

I had a child
when I was a child,

when I was a bartender and lifeguard
patrolling the jetties of others' drownings.

The beach is my stage now,
with horizon as backdrop.

I rise from a sandy audience
and walk across the threshold.

A trespasser among actors,
I become an actor, I become buoyant.

I don't exit left or right.
Rather, I exit behind, into the ocean.

I swim straight out
to another type of audience, the sharks.

They watch the events from a different angle,
and quickly make a martyr of me.

of sharks)

(Silhouettes

THISISNOMOVI

This is The Only Chance You'll Have at Real Life

Move Like This | **Ric Wilson, Terrace Martin**

Because an audience fully alive has the power of payback.
Because it's impossible to add up Los Angeles, a ditty
and the waterfall of the deepest place.
Because guilt diminishes us all.

In *Love Bomb*, Thaïs asks Adonis for a movie.
But not any movie. A blue movie.

Blue and the rose, because on certain nights
the naked body is so desperate,
so exactly bad, badass, and sassy.
Blue and the green of each window.

Characters need names even if they're interchangeable.
Same for viruses.
Same for beaches.
From the beginning Adonis told lies to create new worlds.

Because to remain in the real world is the real cruelty,
the real betrayal of any devotion.
Thaïs keeps fainting. Nico is gone.
It's difficult not to spoil what one prays to.

I have forgotten my mask, and my face was in it.

—Kenneth Patchen,

"JOURNAL OF ALBION MOONLIGHT"

Summertime | Louis Armstrong, Ella Fitzgerald

Gasp
Applause

(((Laughter)))

I am a con man	*I am the supreme being*	*I am an immortal species*
I am an otaku	*I am the offspring of a myrrh tree*	*I am a sex worker turned nun*
I am a race car driver	*I am a fallen angel*	*I am a hydra*

BUSINESS MAN VS. HR WOMAN
MC: DERMOT HUSSEY

AUDIENCE: YOU

LOBBY BAR   RESTROOMS

ENTRANCE/EXIT

| *Heartbeats (Live)* | The Knife |

Revelation of Selene (as Narrator)

Woman is a Word | **Empress Of**

In *Love Bomb*, a new character emerges: moi! Selene.
Adonis is once again swept away. But is it too late?
My voice is a phonograph.
My eyes: Palladian windows.

I want every interaction to be sublime,
to possess an extreme heaviness, or lightness—
to possess the weight of a near-death experience.
For me, to love is to risk everything.

I channel my opera into a cantor,
my saliva into a potent lava.

I don't wait or invite.
I initiate and set the rhythm.
The rhythm of ritualized exchanges.
The rhythm of remission and eruption.

I make Adonis cum inside me.
I raise the kink above his comfort zone.
He can't just show up banal, empty-handed.
He has to arrive precisely, puissant.

(Silhouette

pole

dancing)

LIAR QUIZ

Crimewave (Crystal Castles Vs.) (David Wolf Edit) | **HEALTH**

(Business Man vs. HR Woman: East Coast Edition)

ANNOUNCER: (Offstage) Welcome to Liar Quiz! This show is dedicated to the art of lying truthfully, and with empathy, in a world of fake news, and base propaganda. So, sit back and listen, and see if you can discern fact from fiction. One liar is sitting in the secret square. The contestant that picks it first could win an extravagant, Parisian holiday for two. Which liar is it? Adonis, Nico, Thaïs, the Devil, God, The Two Beasts, Rich Man, Enzo, or the Roach? Here is the master of ceremonies, Dermot Hussey. (Applause)

HUSSEY: Thank you. Thank you very much. Good evening. Welcome, once again, to Liar Quiz. (To the liars) Hello liars!

LIARS: (In unison) Hello Dermot.

HUSSEY: Our first contestant is a business man from Franklin Lakes, New Jersey, a husband, and father of two. (To Business Man) Good evening.

BUSINESS MAN: Good evening.

HUSSEY: The lovely lady to my left is from Brooklyn, New York. Gentrification grows there faster than anywhere else. Please welcome, HR Woman. (Applause)

HR WOMAN: Thank you, Dermot. Glad to be here.

HUSSEY: (To HR Woman) Are you married?

HR WOMAN: No, I am not.

HUSSEY: Married to the job, I guess. (Laughter)

HR WOMAN: You could say that.

HUSSEY: To review, for the forgetful folks at home, the object for the contestants is to get three squares in a row, either across, up and down, or diagonally. It is up to them to figure out if the liars are giving them a truthful answer, or not. That's how they win the squares. Every victory is worth ten trips to the ER, or two tickets to Broadway. And of course, secret squares— there's one in every game—are worth much more. Business Man, you're up first.

BUSINESS MAN: I'd like to start with Rich Man.

HUSSEY: (To Rich Man) True or false? You can cheat on your taxes, sexually harass women, openly brag about it, lose the popular vote, and still become president of the United States of America.

RICH MAN: Well...not if you lose the popular vote. (Gasp)

HUSSEY: Stop now! Enough is enough. Is it true or false?

RICH MAN: That's false.

BUSINESS MAN: I agree.

HUSSEY: No sir. That's actually true. None of those things matter, apparently. Put an O up there. Ok, HR Woman, your turn.

HR WOMAN: Let's go with God.

HUSSEY: Dear God. According to Ashley Madison, the online cheating site, what percentage of married women, who engaged in an affair, reported a "happier marriage" after the affair?

GOD: 100%! (Laughter)

HUSSEY: Seriously now, what percentage of married women reported a happier marriage after an affair? 25%? 33%? 50%?

GOD: Every affair is like a box of chocolate. (Opens a box of chocolate) I'm going to say 50%.

HR WOMAN: I disagree. After my last affair, I didn't go back to my husband. (Gasp)

HUSSEY: (Laughing) Yes, you are right to disagree. 25% report a happier marriage. And I say, that's not all bad. Put another O up there. Back to you, Business Man.

BUSINESS MAN: The Roach for the block.

HUSSEY: (To Business Man) Yes, that makes sense. (To Roach) The book, *The Hero With A Thousand Faces*, was written by which author? Stan Lee? Joseph Campbell? Or Joseph Heller?

ROACH: How would I know? I never see faces. Only heels. (Laughter) But I do read a lot. And this book in particular is one of my all-time favorites.

HUSSEY: (To Business Man) He sounds confident. What about you? Do you read a lot?

BUSINESS MAN: No, never. But I've seen all the Avengers' movies.

HUSSEY: Roach, tell us, who is the author?

ROACH: Stan Lee, creator of Spiderman and many other superheroes.

HUSSEY: (To Business Man) Do you agree?

BUSINESS MAN: Yes, I do.

HUSSEY: You shouldn't. Joseph Campbell is the author. And that means HR Woman is our winner! (Theme music) We're going to take a quick break for commercial, and will be right back. (Cut to commercial)

(Behind the squares.)

ROACH: (To Thaïs) I love lying to suits in leather shoes.

THAÏS: (To Roach) That's my ex-husband. (Smirking) And they're faux leather.

HUSSEY: (Internally) Occasionally, liars tell the truth accidentally. Strange to admit these accidents do not reveal or negate their lies. What is truth then?

Dawn

500 Days of Summer | Grady

(February 2020, NYC)

Gone last night new museum date
oh this chill
of waking too early
these cold shivers these neon-toned

day-glo nightmares of the 60s and 70s

of corrupt brutality. Pop
on a suit and tie because
crime doesn't pay and
riot guards will not punch you in the face

oh this chill. A portrait should

be warm
and light and buoyant
not a heavy safe
morning and second dates, too
same for the horizon
not a sleeve of ice
or a blade

Why not a kiss? (Selene's kiss)

Verlaine

LAVENDER Dounia

The young of the city
they didn't want us around
said we couldn't park there
or join them, but

see, they quickly forget

this is how I see us
olives, wine, Verlaine
every image a good one
a Duchamp

my impulse, forthcoming

windows
opening in humidity
of summer
a perimeter of prayer
and surrender. Drummers on a rooftop
and us. Ah us. Pacific on the inside
not wanting to blow up each other's world

none of it is neat

VERRAZANO

Please Don't Touch (The Golden Filter Remix) | Polly Scattergood

(Nico sits at a piano and begins playing. She talks over her playing.)

These   *boombox*   *a*   *the*
sons   *on*   *low*   *outer*
these   *brownstone*   *yellow*   *boroughs*
sons   *giant*   *moon*   *the*
fall   *steps*   *between*   *of-*
burning   *on*   *the*   *ends*
into   *giant*   *bridge's*   *ends-*
nonbeing   *stairs*   *towers*   *of*
into   *these*   *blazing*   *their*
being   *sons*   *the*   *dreaming*
into   *climbing*   *trans*   *their*
bebop   *the*   *narrows*   *acting*
rhythm   *entire*   *fog*   *out*
and   *night*   *lit*   *these*
blues   *of*   *passage*   *sons*
a   *always*   *joining*   *fallin'*

NICO: (To Adonis) Do you hear what I'm playing?

The   *its*   *to*
world   *history*   *this*
of   *leading*   *moment*

ADONIS: The world is a nor'easter.

(Nico keeps playing.)

NICO: Y o u d o n ' t l o v e m e
Y o u
l o v e
t h e
i d e a
o f
m e

(Nico gets up from the piano, goes to the window, opens it, and climbs out onto the fire escape. She ascends to the roof on a cast iron ladder. Adonis hesitantly follows her, each rung battering the soles of his bare feet. When he reaches the rooftop, Nico is gone. He doesn't see any way down but the way they came up. There are no nearby roofs at a similar or safe height to jump down to. Bewildered, defeated, with his feet aching, he sits down on the damp tar. The sun begins to rise and spread its light on the city.)

Of Sirens

You Don't Love Me (No, No, No)-Extended Mix | Dawn Penn

I'm falling in/out of
blindness, losing altitude
my guilt, oh god
you don't love me, no
no, no, if I were innocent, there'd be
no us, what am I saying?
I did more for you out of guilt
than love, I hand you a gun
I take the word love
out of your mouth

Funeral Home

Yannis and the Dragon | Christodoulos Halaris

I didn't look in the coffin
I looked at the moon
between the bridge's towers
it was a full, yellow moon
there was a haze developing
it hid the other side
traffic disappeared into it

a cinder block in my chest
anchored me
to my backrest
the bridge was expanding
it breached the room
its lights stabbed my eyes
its cars pounded me in the face

even a bridge is a betrayal
all reality is mute
I want most of all to finish
a playlist but my migraine!
I can't search any more songs
to send (accuse?) her:
my mother passed away

BRIEFEST SCENE IN A HOTEL LOBBY

Company | Tinashe

(Nico and Adonis sit across from each other.)

NICO: Just because there are helium heart balloons you think people are in love. What is love in your dialect?

ADONIS: Coitus. Ethanol. Cafe noir. Pepper. (Adonis prostrates himself.)

NICO: You're such a haunt.

(Enter Thaïs.)

ADONIS: (Rising) I haunt. I grovel. I'm merely ready with answers.

THAÏS: (To Nico) Did you expect other exploits?

ADONIS: (To Thaïs) Thaïs, my bride.

(Enter the Devil.)

NICO: (To Thaïs) No. I expected... (To Adonis) Hamilton tickets.

DEVIL: Let's, all of us, go to the park.

THAÏS: The park?

NICO: The horror.

ADONIS: Yes, the park!

DEVIL: It's perfect! We can stay up all night and howl at the moon. Then we can watch the sun rise through the trees. In the morning we can find a cave to sleep the powerful sleep of vampires. When we wake up, we'll be several years younger. And more attractive. For breakfast, which would be dinner-time for the uninitiated, we can drink from each other. I'll bring arak to rinse our palates. We can build an effigy of god from twigs. A crude figure. Then light it on fire and watch the embers snuff out the stars.

NICO: No thanks.

THAÏS: I'll pass.

ADONIS: I'll go.

(Nico removes her waist beads and returns them to Adonis.)

NICO: (To Adonis) I'm starting over. Thanks for the playlists. And the nipple clamps.

ADONIS: (Receiving the waist beads) You're welcome. Thank you. And I'm sorry, you know, about the Whitney... I misunderstood.

NICO: Me too.

THAÏS: (Clearing her throat) Well now...

(Exit Nico.)

DEVIL: And then there were three.

THAÏS: No. (Showing the Devil out) Not tonight.

(Exit Devil. Thaïs returns to Adonis, takes the waist beads from him, and drops them in a nearby waste bin.)

ADONIS: Parks are infantile, after all.

THAÏS: (Pressing the elevator button) Infantile, yes.

(The elevator arrives. The doors open. They get on.)

ADONIS: I'm an idiot, I know.

THAÏS: Well, you are capable of idiocy, you've proven that.

(The elevator doors close. Thaïs presses a button.)

ADONIS: It was just that... You were sick... I was missing what we had, what we became to each other, that feeling I would get when we would meet, the nervousness, the excitement... All of it. I liked sneaking around the city with you. It became a new city... I was chasing that!

(The elevator doors open.)

THAÏS: (Stepping out) I liked the sneaking around too, when it was with me.

ADONIS: (Following) I'll make it up to you.

THAÏS: (Grinning) Yes, you will.

The Man Who Saw The Counterfactual

Legend In His Own Mind | Gil Scott-Heron

It was difficult for him
to stay on the straight and narrow
even when walking in line
his eyes wandered off to admire a heart-shaped butt
his ears hung back to eavesdrop on strangers
his nose mounted a far-off flower
his mouth drove to a karaoke bar
his hands stole away to peel an orange
his cock buried itself in the dry hot sand
his spine swam in a lake of blooming algae

Every Sunday
he'd call his bits and pieces back
and say, Stay put. Love the one before you
in your wholeness as bridegroom.
I know. I do. I will, he'd answer himself
but then he'd glimpse a window
green from the diffusion of inside light with sunlight
and he'd see into that window
what no one else could see
and it wasn't what he saw that made him happy

sometimes it was great sorrow but it was sexy too
and it beckoned him

The Making of a Collage (Of Collages)

I cannot sleep because lustful thoughts of you—
I put on an old lover's playlist. Distant Dream.

I begin a collage. Eyes emerge as a theme.
There is looking, and looking back, and then—

where art emerges—looking back at the looking back.
I feel my nipples softening against my thermal shirt.

This collage will be double-sided.
I have a weakness for backsides.

Making love is not the same as fucking.
Except for me: it is! But don't be afraid.

My love is not a prison.
More like wind. Or, a cool breeze.

I inhabit my absence on side A.
I insert myself on side B. That's me twenty years ago.

And that's me as a centaur,
afflicted by the Androcephalous Syndrome.

I could love you. More than once a month.
I could love you like an ambulance,

that is, if you want saving. Or, I could love you
like a hearse, if you want to say to the world,

Fuck you. Fuck you!
The way a volcano says to the moon.

ROACH

Good Pussy | **Alia Kadir**

(Roach visits a sullen Adonis.)

ROACH: You idiot! Did you think she loved you?

ADONIS: No. Of course not. I thought…

ROACH: You did! You thought she was falling for you.

ADONIS: No. It's just that… The way she was… It felt like something special, you know… At times, at least.

ROACH: You really are a moron. It wasn't you she loved. It was her job.

ADONIS: Huh…

ROACH: (Apologetic) You miss her.

ADONIS: Yeah. What happened? Is she ok?

ROACH: Yes, she's fine. One of her so-called friends outed her.

ADONIS: What?! Why?! What an asshole!

ROACH: Jealousy, revenge, who knows?

ADONIS: Fuck!

ROACH: Forced into early retirement. Not easy for her.

ADONIS: Not easy for me either. I loved her.

ROACH: (Sucking teeth) Just when I thought you couldn't get any dumber. You didn't love her.

ADONIS: I did!

ROACH: No. You loved the feeling of surrendering to her. You loved being swept away.

ADONIS: Hm. (Enter Nico.)

NICO: (To Adonis) 'The blooming algae, although deadly, imbued a magnificent green.' (Smiling) Are you impressed?

ADONIS: (To Nico) Yes, very! I'm so glad you're ok. I was worried. I miss you terribly.

NICO: Do you still want a blurb?

ADONIS: You got my texts?

NICO: This book is a mature book. For mature audiences. The author owes me $400.

ADONIS: (Paying her) Thank you!

NICO: Now, I will travel far away from here.

ROACH: The goodbye without insult has been accomplished.

(Exit Nico. Enter Selene.)

Peyton's Play Pen (Reprise)

Serial Lover | Kehlani

I who am desirable return
I have no sense of gifts

I spoil my goodness with poor timing
I am the least violent lover

My instinct is to last
I utter my own diminishment

I describe my forgetfulness
As belonging to the future

I love more than I am loved
This is not blackmail

This is bondage
A tramp tattoo

I'm afraid how you see me
The gesture of stripping

I exit a different door than I entered
Onto a different street

In this way I glanced off you
Yes I can fall in love with anyone

(Not) The World

The world is a place where it's forbidden
to love freely,
fully...

The world is for prudes only,
the police of all nations.

Let's go to Union Hotel,
or Oscar Wilde, or Play Pen. Anywhere!
Only not the world.

SELENE

Sugar on My Tongue | Talking Heads

SELENE: All my exes were dicks. None of them wanted to be in an open relationship.

ADONIS: Too jealous?

SELENE: Too proud.

ADONIS. Hmph.

SELENE: I have to tell you something. I have a massive crush on you, it's insane.

ADONIS: I feel the same! You should know... (Selene kisses him, shutting him up impermanently.) I am not a top. I am not a bottom. I am not a dick, I assure you. I am not an ass, either. What I am is a tongue. Not your tongue. That is yours. Not my tongue. That would imply a me in this instance. What I am is a sex toy that you own that is a tongue. Put me on your clit. And I will be a tongue... Put me on your asshole. And I will be a tongue... Put me on your nipples. And I will be a tongue... Put me on the soles of your feet. And I will be a tongue... Put me on your armpits. And I will be a tongue... Put me on your neck. And I will be a tongue... Put me on your clit once more. And I will be a tongue... Put me on your mouth. And I will be a tongue. (Adonis muffles her moaning with his mouth, inhaling her exhalations.)

SELENE: (Internally) I am sugar.

The Wearing of a Mask (Of Masks)

Masquerade | Clan of Xymox

I'm wearing my mother's death on my mouth.
In my hands, I have my wallet and a package for Thaïs.
I walk with a slight limp, imperceptible to others,
but for me, I feel a pinch with every step.
My breath turns back on itself, rejected by the world.
Somehow, I have become more polluted.
"What is it you need?" The man in the Post Office asks.
A time made out of poetry and sky. Like that day in LA.
Love was more urgent then. Now it's more uncertain.
I'm surprised when anyone loves me back.
Suddenly I feel ill. A dizziness comes over me.
I hear in the birds' chirping, my mother's name:
Evie, Evie, Evie... My cousin made me this mask.
Inside the heart, she put my mother's death date.
Or you could say, around my mother's death, she stitched a heart.

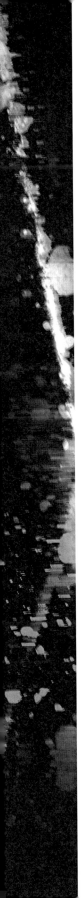

The Grand Dispersal

Mysterium Tremendum | Christopher Young

1.

The sea wasn't calm. But I knew
I could swim in the currents.
I wasn't afraid of drowning.
I was afraid of the glare from the sun.

I curled up on the floor, because not-dying hurts.
Others too share this beautiful pain.

Many homes now have empty beds. [Hum of electricity.]
The faces on screen overlap my reflection.

There is still the beach and its currents.
From heaven, I must look like I'm drowning.

Their entire dying reduced to a quarantine
among strangers, caught in their own not-dying.

A cruel magic trick: the first to die
don't actually die. They just disappear.
Like sirens into a distance.
An immeasurable distance.

2.

A child mistaken for an ambulance wails in the night.
They say the good go to heaven, and look down on us,
            and protect us.

In dying, they say, at least there is an end to the suffering.
A divine type of mercy. A final gift.

840,000 souls have been extended this mercy.
Yet the world keeps being shredded by plain horror.

840,000 souls in makeshift freezers waiting for the ground to thaw,
with hope the disease will become a cure.

I can't cry, so I lick my eyes.
I see my mother in a dream, and I run to her.

They say, Everything is back to normal,
And, Nothing is the same.

There's a world out there that is happy. It's just not here.
Here, they scowl, the Rich Man is king!

No one believes they'll die.
No one wears a mask.

BRAIN MRI

Cherry-coloured Funk | Cocteau Twins

(Adonis drifts off. He dreams of Nico.)

NICO: Your chest hair is so perfect. It's as if someone painted it on you.

ADONIS: Your eyes are so vast, and green. Not a naïve green, no. The green of earth. The green of an optimism that persists even after loss. An optimism defined by sunrise. But not just any sunrise, every sunrise.

NICO: You have a way with words. And your tongue, when you go down on me. That thing you do, with tongue and finger.

ADONIS: The way I can talk to you. When I'm with you, I can't stop from opening up.

NICO: Don't worry, I'll handle your secrets delicately.

ADONIS: Actually, I'm worried about how I'll see the world, how I'll take in every sunrise, from this point on.

NICO: A few years from now, you won't even remember me.

ADONIS: (Caressing Nico) No. For me, remembering is easier than forgetting. (Staring into Nico's eyes) Somewhere, someone is seeing snow for the first time. And someone else, who has seen it a thousand times, is watching them.

(A technician logs diagnostic images of Adonis' brain.)

[Snow. Static. Fade out.]

Tomorrow

Tomorrow I will jump off the Verrazano.
I will slow my car to a stop in the right lane.
I will struggle to climb the railing
and balance myself against the wind gusts.
Traffic will whiz by, narrowly avoiding my car.
Eventually, a police car with muted sirens will pull up.

Tomorrow I will jump off the Verrazano.
The air will feel liquid.
The lights will reveal my tormented face.
All my friends and family will see me for the first time,
falling with no sense of proportion.
Turn, look at me, see what you have made of me!

Tomorrow I will jump off the Verrazano
and survive the fall.
I will die on the way to the hospital.
Although I will be misunderstood—
since I am guilty of this—
all my friends and family will see me!

Tomorrow I will jump off the Verrazano.
Everything will be solemn, gray.
I will cut my hair, shave.
Still, it will be a closed coffin.
My friends will sneak a pair of aces onto my chest.
A wobbly story, told and retold, is what I'll become.

Adonis the Syndrome

Moody Blues | Nights in White Satin (Single Version)

Adonis the virus

Adonis the werewolf

Adonis the worker man

Adonis the zeitgeist

Adonis the accomplice

Adonis the actor

Adonis the bartender

Adonis the bridegroom

Adonis the bull's eye

Adonis the centaur

Adonis the center square

Adonis the cheater

Adonis the cormorant

Adonis the doppelganger

Adonis the double orgasm

Adonis the face

Adonis the father

Adonis the fuck

Adonis the gun on wall

Adonis the handle

Adonis the heel

Adonis the infected nucleus

Adonis the invocation

Adonis the john

Adonis the kilroy

Adonis the liar

Adonis the lifeguard

Adonis the lover

Adonis the martyr

Adonis the mosquito

Adonis the nude

Adonis the patron

Adonis the poet

Adonis the portrait

Adonis the prisoner

This is the arrow

Adonis the question mark
Adonis the rock
Adonis the smuggler
Adonis the son
Adonis the squid
Adonis the swan dive—

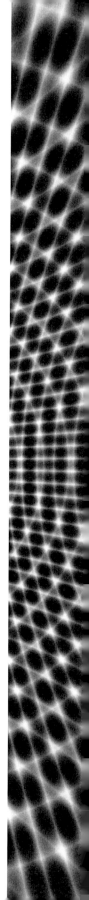

ADONIS GIVES A READING (ALTERNATE ENDING)

My Angel | **Horace Andy**

ADONIS: (Applause) Now, my newest poem, Paperback Hotel, or, Tiny Coffin.

Even here, in light, fatigue jerks the heart, between a breeze
and ruffling papers; like verses her mind catalogs
piously, humming, towards some future, self-fulfilling doom; his
poems mutely boxed, burrowing
through every hotel of hallucination
where desire, unhinged from sleep
can play out, is played out, in waking dreams.
This is the last of your wedding gifts,
not to be opened until your divorce; (Looking up)
then you can go to Paris, or Seoul, or Lima.

(Richard shoves through the crowd and pulls out a gun.)

RICHARD: (Pointing the gun at Adonis) You fuck. You ruined my promotion.

ADONIS: What are you talking about? I thought it was in the bag. A done deal.

RICHARD: No! The higher ups rejected my paperwork.

ADONIS: God has a sense of humor, after all.

GOD: (From the audience) Ha!

RICHARD: It's all your fault. I blame you. You ruined everything. You made me look bad. Worse, you made me pout.

ADONIS: But you had Ellen in your back pocket. That wasn't enough?

RICHARD: Obviously not. She's useless.

ELLEN: (Gasping) Richard! I can't believe you. (She storms off)

RICHARD: (To Adonis) You fuck! (He points his gun at him...but he doesn't shoot.)

BUSINESS MAN: (To Richard) Enough! Are you going to shoot him or what!? (Richard lowers his gun, then chases after Ellen.) What a clown! (He reveals his own gun, and steadily aims it at Adonis.) This is for stealing my wife's heart, and filling her head with delusions of happiness.

ADONIS: Wait. (The Business Man shoots Adonis in the chest repeatedly, until he is pulled away by Lady in Fine Hat. They run off.)

THAÏS: No! No! No! (Adonis falls down bleeding profusely onto the floor. Thaïs desperately tries to stop the bleeding.)

GOD: (Snacking on popcorn) I misread Richard. Hmph.

THAÏS: (To God) Fuck you!

GOD: (To Thaïs) But your ex... I have to admit, I admire him.

(Chaos. Sirens. First responders arrive. They struggle to pry Adonis' body from Thaïs.)

Be Summer, Thaïs

Summer 2020 | Jhené Aiko

Be summer, Thaïs
That your hands may unfold
And bees suckle at your fingertips

Be a lake, Thaïs
That frogs may kiss your forehead
And giant firs guard your meditation

Be a hot air balloon, Thaïs
That your feet may graze every summit
And snow leopards cushion your layovers

Be a bridge, Thaïs
That your eyes may see through fog
Into the depths of oceans
Into the stomachs of whales

Be a totem and dildo, Thaïs
That your sighs, however soft
However loud, may funnel the winds
And all creatures be touched by your cool breeze

Portrait of Adonis (by Nico)

Angel of the Morning | Juice Newton

Adonis saw Nico as an artist
of limitless creativity, a goddess of all things
that cannot be measured or summarized.

Some call this death.
Some call it life. Mere words
for dreams that do not expire.

Nico wrote Adonis,
Send me a poem, and he sent her
a line from Lispector.

Nico wrote Adonis,
Send me a glare, and he sent her
a box of paints, glitter.

Nico wrote Adonis,
in response to a question
he had yet to ask, Yes,

and from this he learned
how to make art from the unspoken,
how to give and receive a gift.

Adonis once said to Nico,
Give me courage, and
the ability to see in all things

their beauty, or
if not yet flourished, the seed.
Nico painted him a watercolor.

A KILROY THANKSGIVING

Go To Town | Doja Cat

(Beach)

ADONIS: How did you end up here?

(Adonis and Enzo are playing chess. The Devil is surfing.)

ENZO: I did my research.

ADONIS: I'm impressed.

ENZO: Don't get carried away. It's not all sex and drugs, and chess.

ADONIS: You were never that good at chess.

ENZO: Ha. You sucked at life.

ADONIS: Life is exhausting.

ENZO: You need to leave New York.

ADONIS: I could come here. Move in with you.

ENZO: You'd have to divorce your wife.

ADONIS: She doesn't believe in divorce.

ENZO: Just torture.

ADONIS: I enjoy being tortured.

DEVIL: (Throwing down his surfboard) Kilroys! What's for lunch?

ENZO: Ouzo.

DEVIL: The last time I drank ouzo, I woke up in a shopping cart, in the middle of the desert.

ADONIS: Burning Man.

DEVIL: Burning Man! You've got to come. One time, come on.

ENZO: I prefer bowling alone.

ADONIS: I prefer a pillow and mattress.

DEVIL: (Pouring ouzo into three plastic cups) A toast. To my fellow Kilroys, may you choose immediate gratification over eternal life.

ENZO: Cent'Amanti.

ADONIS: Yes. (They drink.)

DEVIL: (Lying down) As ego goes down, empathy goes up. As empathy goes up, dogma goes down. As dogma goes down, open-mindedness goes up. As open-mindedness goes up, taboos go down. As taboos go down, creativity goes up—more so for the curious-minded. And as creativity goes up, so does art, so does lovemaking, so do mutual orgasms.

ENZO: Un caso per un'estate senza fine.

Gazebo Beach

Connan Mockasin

I Wanna Roll With You

The world is full of loss.

Intermissions of laughter. Sighing.

Not-crying. Thaïs, dearest Thaïs,

thank you for the portable typewriter.

Spare yourself the heavy finds.

Your gifts override the clouds.

What is the name of the food truck by the lake?

Who stays in that hotel?

Why Nico? And why tell you? I don't know.

Where is the photo of us in the rain,

in front of The Flying Lobster?

Your umbrella flowered by wind.

Langston Hughes lived nearby, briefly.

I can take you there. Please, yes!

Intersections of escape and harvest.

Also, a Hollywood film with Morgan Freeman.

I reach out to her.

She puts my hands back on my hips.

I tilt my head back,

upward to a tree bleeding sap.

I kneel down into my body

to see the ground and in the ground

myself. I reset my balance

against a dizzying world. A world full of patterns

and no-patterns.

No-patterns wins out!

Before and after the conversation

where I moronically ask for a blurb.

In the sky, above the tree line:
a milkman flying on a bike, shirtless.
The film features a young Adonis.
Who is real? Who are actors?
The record player plays a wedding song.
She speaks: my heart hatches.
She speaks: instructions for escape.
A guide I don't recognize as a saint.
A guide I mistake for a con.
The smartphone streams a playlist,
To Fuck To. Yes, that's the one.
I go down, crossing several thresholds: belly,
belly button, waist beads, piercings.
To bury my head in the world.
To play sand in an hourglass.
To hold my breath underwater until I pass out.
And then to wait to be saved by someone.
Someone I am trusting my life to.
Someone I have been trusting my life to
in regular intervals.
Intermissions of summer
in seasons of depleting sun.
It's useless to ask how something died.
The answer will not bring it back to life.
Thaïs is a lake.
Nico: a portrait of the protagonist, in character.

What if I were the milkman?
Not the milkman, the paperboy!
Not the paperboy, the madam boss!
I'm thinking that is the role for me.
Not that of the husband.

(Birthday) Love Poem for Selene

Birthday Sex | Jeremih

You have to be patient with me.
I beg you.
I'm a late bloomer.

The dawn unfolds slowly for me.
Eventually, I'll compliment
your curvature

without shaking or clumsiness.
I can be your flagpole,
or your sail (with mast).

If only you bless me with time,
and rendezvous.
For me, no two utterances,

not even the same word,
the same sentence, are the same.
No two flowers,

however identical, are the same,
smell the same,
react the same in one's hands,

even in the same hands.
No two kisses are comparable or separable.
They stem from a line

of kissing that is in fact the same kiss,
continuing in its mode.
This is how I beg you to receive my kisses,

my touch, my lofty cock.
It will only grow firmer, steadier,
reach deeper into you,

in time, in recurrence,
dilating your G spot,
and your tight anus.

LOVE BOMB

The Man Who Couldn't Afford to Orgy | **John Cale**

(Beach)

(35 mm film)

1.

> Exterior: 1950s, suburbs.
> Interior: Bedroom.

A man (HUSBAND) and woman (WIFE) sleep as an alarm goes off. The man gets up, showers, gets dressed (suit and tie). He has difficulty choosing between two ties. He asks his wife to pick one. She picks one.

WIFE: Good luck with your interview today.

HUSBAND: Thank you.

He walks outside toward the driveway where his car is parked. The milk man (MILK MAN) is approaching and they wave hello to each other. As he starts his car, he sees the paperboy (PAPERBOY) riding his bike down the block making the morning deliveries. He pulls onto the road and, at the first intersection, passes the mail man (MAIL MAN) in his mail truck. He drives another block before stopping at a red light. While stopped, he looks in his rearview mirror and adjusts his tie. He is dissatisfied with the tie. He makes a U-turn.

As he approaches his house, he sees the milk carton cart on his porch, the paperboy's bike lying on its side on his lawn, and the mail truck parked in front of his house.

He walks into his house loosening his tie. He sees men's shoes strewn on the floor. He slowly walks to his bedroom, and nudges the door open, slightly.

His wife is standing nude in the middle of the milk man, paperboy, and mail man. They are barefoot and shirtless. They encircle her in a group hug.

He quietly falls to one knee. He palms the floor to keep his balance. He watches.

The men begin to massage and kiss her shoulders and whisper in her ears. She is standing there with her eyes closed enjoying their hands and mouths on her. They massage and lick her from the top down, taking their time with each section of her body, first the neck and shoulders, then her breasts, biceps, and upper back, then her stomach, lower back, and sides just above her hips, then her pussy, and ass, fingers and tongues teasing tenderly, then her quads and hamstrings, then her knees and calves, then her Achilles tendons, her ankles, the tops of her feet, fingers in-between her toes. She is moaning sweetly. When they finish with her feet, they stand up and remove their pants in near unison.

HUSBAND: No!

He faints, falling into the room. At first, they all look at him quizzically, then they go to him, to resuscitate him.

WIFE: He needs air. Take off his clothes.

They remove his clothes. He regains consciousness.

HUSBAND: Why?

WIFE: I am filled with desire. We all are. Even you.

HUSBAND: But I love you.

WIFE: You love the idea of me. I am an acceptable form of your desire.

HUSBAND: I don't understand.

WIFE: Stand up.

The husband now stands in the middle and the four of them encircle him. His wife faces him and initiates the group massage with a kiss on his lips...

This time when they finish with his feet, they lie him down on the floor, on his back. They straighten and spread his arms and legs so that he looks like an X on the floor. The wife kneels between his legs. Positioning herself on her knees and elbows, she presses down on his groin with her hands, thumbing his testicles, while taking his cock in her mouth. The paperboy kneels behind her, and on his knees and elbows, he fingers her clitoris while licking her ass. The mail man and milk man kiss his nipples, straddling his arms and lifting his hands to stroke their cocks. This goes on until the husband orgasms.

WIFE: Now we have to get you to that interview!

They all dress quickly and run out of the house. They choose the mail truck over the car. They get in, and the mail man drives them to the husband's interview. During the drive, the wife is adjusting the husband's tie, licking her hand and setting his hair.

2.

> Exterior: Office building, parking lot.
> Interior: Executive office, reception area.

They recklessly park in a reserved parking spot and rush into the building.

RECEPTIONIST: Who is the interviewee?

They all point to the husband.

RECEPTIONIST: Ok, you (gesturing to the husband) come with me. The rest of you wait here. And don't touch anything.

She leads him down a hallway and brings him into an executive office. She introduces him to her boss, Madam Boss (MADAM BOSS), and then exits.

MADAM BOSS: You look surprised.

HUSBAND: I was expecting a man.

MADAM BOSS: Would you prefer to work for a man?

HUSBAND: No, no. I would like to work for you.

Meanwhile, in the reception area:

The wife, milk man, paperboy, and mail man are sitting in the reception area eying the receptionist (RECEPTIONIST). She is busily typing.

MAIL MAN: Excuse me. Did you receive your mail today?

RECEPTIONIST: No, not yet.

MAIL MAN: I think I have something for you. It's a group hug. Would you like a group hug from me and my friends?

RECPTIONIST: Um, ok. I guess I could use a hug. But gentle.

MAIL MAN: Absolutely.

The receptionist stands up and comes out from behind her desk. They encircle her. The mail man faces her and initiates the group hug. It slowly evolves into a group massage. He narrates the proceedings:

MAIL MAN: This is an eight-hander. Remember, friends, be gentle. Let's work the temples, and around the ears. You smell so nice. Let's skip over the neck and work the outer shoulders, the upper arms, and softly the upper back. Let's skip over the breasts—

RECEPTIONIST: No! Don't skip over the breasts.

MAIL MAN: Ok, let's focus on her breasts, and her armpits, above her blouse, and her belly, and her lower back, her hips, let's loosen her blouse, go under her blouse, return to her breasts, over her bra, under her bra, let's remove her bra (her bra drops to the floor), palms, knuckles, and forearms on skin, fingertips on nipples, across her belly, graze her belly button, let's go back down to her hips and ass, over her skirt, let's impress our faces in her ass and groin, let's reach up under her skirt, over her underwear, under her underwear, let's remove her underwear (the wife pulls the receptionist's underwear down to the floor, the receptionist lifts one foot then the other to step out of her underwear and also flips off her shoes in the process), let's focus on her thighs, let's unbutton her skirt, let's remove her skirt (her skirt falls abruptly to the floor), let's kiss her midsection, her ass and pussy while massaging her thighs, let's work our mouths down her thighs while letting our hands linger, let's nibble on her shins and calves, no bite marks though, let's lick the tops of her feet, the tops of her toes.

The receptionist stands nude, her head arched back, her eyes closed but skyward, touching her own breast with one hand, and her pussy with the other. The others at her feet, kissing them. She is a tree and they are her roots. She is a statue and they are her foundation of misshapen stone. In near unison, they all stand up and remove their clothes.

They lie the receptionist down on the floor, on her back. They straighten and spread her arms and legs so that she looks like an X on the floor. The wife kneels between her legs. Positioning herself on her knees and elbows, she presses down on the receptionist's groin with her hands while thumbing and licking her clitoris. The paperboy kneels behind the wife and inserts his cock in her pussy. The mail man and milk man kiss the receptionist's nipples, straddling her arms and lifting her hands to stroke their cocks. This goes on until everyone, except the receptionist, gets up and repositions themselves. The wife straddles the receptionist's face, facing away from her body. The paperboy kneels between the receptionist's legs and, lifting her legs, inserts his cock in her pussy. The milk man stands in front of the wife and she takes his cock in her mouth while holding his quads. The mail man stands in front of the paperboy, over the receptionist, and inserts his cock into the paperboy's mouth while holding the back of his head. The milk man places his hands on the shoulders of the mail man, balancing the group. Occasionally, the back of the wife's head bumps the mail man's ass. This goes on until they all orgasm.

In the executive office, the interview proceeds:

HUSBAND: I don't have any managerial experience, no. But I'm good with people. I get along with everybody.

MADAM BOSS: A friend to all?

HUSBAND: Yes.

MADAM BOSS: No. Not to all. Not all the time. Are you going to let them walk all over you?

HUSBAND: Well, no, of course not.

MADAM BOSS: I am not convinced—

At this point, the wife, milk man, paperboy, mail man, and receptionist barge into the room merrily.

MADAM BOSS: What is going on?!

RECEPTIONIST: Madam Boss, I'm sorry, but you need a group hug.

MADAM BOSS: Who are these (gesturing to the wife, milk man, paperboy, and mail man) naked heathens?!

RECEPTIONIST: They are a love bomb sent from heaven.

HUSBAND: She's right! It's true. I found them fucking my wife this morning. At first, I fainted. Then they fucked me and drove me to this interview. Once they fuck you, part of you dies, but another, more magnificent part is born.

MADAM BOSS: You're all crazy. I'm calling security. (She picks up the phone and dials security) Hello, security? Please come to my office immediately. There are several intruders here. (She hangs up the phone)

The nude mass seems unfazed. They are still glowing in the afterglow of their lovemaking. They appear more beautiful than earlier. Not so much in appearance as in how they move and look at each other. It's subtle but noticeable. Madam Boss is noticing it too.

MADAM BOSS: Security will be here any second.

The husband takes out a pack of cigarettes and begins passing it around. They each take one but none of them have a lighter. They see a lighter on Madam Boss' desk. They gesture towards the lighter. She nods her approval. The husband lights his cigarette first, removes his jacket, and gives both his jacket and lighter to his wife. She puts on the jacket, which she leaves unbuttoned, then lights her cigarette, the paper boy's and the milk man's before passing the lighter to the receptionist. She lights hers and the mail man's.

RECEPTIONIST: (to Madam Boss) Smoke?

MADAM BOSS: Yeah, I guess. What is taking them so long? Why are you all so (she pauses briefly to light her cigarette) calm? Content? (She exhales) So beautiful?

WIFE: We are unafraid. What about you? What are you afraid of?

Security knocks gruffly on the door. Madam boss walks to the door, parting the nude mass, and opens it slightly so security cannot see in.

MADAM BOSS: Never mind. False alarm.

Madam boss closes the door, leans her back on it, and sighs.

MADAM BOSS: I have no one. I need no one. I want no one.

They create a half circle around Madam Boss. Her back is still against the door. They all simultaneously exhale a plume of smoke, which she inhales. The husband collects all the lit cigarettes and extinguishes them in an ashtray on Madam Boss' desk. He returns to the half circle. The others make way for him so that he faces Madam Boss. She steps away from the door and towards him. The others fall in behind her forming a full circle around her. There are no words spoken. Instinctively, they begin their group massage by touching and kissing her temples and ears...

When the husband reaches under her dress and cups the gap between her inner thighs, he is startled momentarily, communicated by a quick glance at Madam Boss' face, but continues without pause, without restraint. The circle drops to their knees.

The husband hikes Madam Boss' skirt above her hips and pulls down her underwear, revealing a large cock which he takes in his mouth...

They undress Madam Boss and lie her down on the floor, on her back. They straighten and spread her arms and legs so that she looks like an X on the floor. The husband kneels between her legs. Positioning himself on his knees and elbows, he presses down on Madam Boss' groin with his hands, thumbing her testicles, while taking her cock in his mouth. The wife and receptionist kiss Madam Boss' nipples, straddling her arms and lifting her hands to stroke their clitorises. The milk man kneels behind the wife, and on his knees and elbows, he fingers her pussy while licking her ass. The mail man kneels behind the receptionist, and on his knees and elbows, he fingers her pussy while licking her ass. The paperboy kneels above Madam Boss, and on his knees and elbows, he cups her ears while kissing her lips upside down. This goes on until the paperboy, husband, milk man, and mail man get up and reposition themselves.

The paperboy straddles Madam Boss' face, facing her body. He slides his cock into her mouth then leans down and takes her cock into his. The paperboy palms the floor to maintain his balance. Madam boss hugs his lower back. The husband kneels between Madam Boss' legs and, lifting her legs slightly, inserts his cock in her ass. The milk man kneels behind the wife and inserts his cock in her ass. The mail man kneels behind the receptionist and inserts his cock in her ass. This goes on until they all orgasm.

Love Bomb | N.E.R.D.

Invocation of the Cock

Hit the Back | King Princess

Have I not invented this pain?
This cock that bends
toward sadness
like a flower made heavy by rain?

This tightness! You'll never get it back.
What is the child to us?
And what does hurt-so-good mean
to you? You frown

at my sensitivity. *Fuck me!*,
you say. *Fuck me harder!*
And I fuck deeper, harder,
with an ear retuned for fucking...

I turn and face the audience (wiping blood
from my cock): *The world is also this.*

Inside the Cock

Eternity | Noah Collette, Sonia Tavik, Kenndoe

i
s

t
h
e

q
u
e
s
t
i
o
n

What
is
your
name?
is
a
tongue
made
of
ocean.
is
a
garden
of
anemones.
is
a
photo
of
Nico
at
the
New
Museum.
is
the
dawn
of
the grand dispersal.

(In the photo Nico is holding up a portrait of Clarice Lispector in front of her face. The portrait is a close-up of Lispector's upper face—nose, eyes, forehead. Nico is holding the portrait in a way that is anatomically aligned with her face, revealing her lips, chin, and neck, giving the illusion of a full face: the top half Lispector's, the bottom half Nico's. It's the only image Adonis has left of Nico.)

RICH MAN

Pretender | **Black Marble**

(Oval Office)

RICH MAN: What are we going to do about this foreign virus?

BUSINESS MAN: Build a wall.

RICH MAN: We did that already. We're doing that. I need something else.

BUSINESS MAN: Keep calling it a hoax.

RICH MAN: We could do that.

CHORUS: (Dancing slowly, waving their arms) What about us? Are we not enough?

RICH MAN: Ick! We're going to need something new.

BUSINESS MAN: I just met with big pharma...

RICH MAN: And? Spit it out.

BUSINESS MAN: They have a vaccine.

RICH MAN: They have a vaccine? Already?!

BUSINESS MAN: Yup. It's not perfect, but it's something. It'll do.

RICH MAN: Hmph! I knew there was a reason I kept you around besides your mother. By the way, how is she these days?

BUSINESS MAN: Ok, tucked away in Palm Beach, sipping mimosas poolside.

RICH MAN: Good... Alright, let's go with the vaccine. Write me a script. Buy stock in it. I'll make an announcement. We'll calm the masses and make a buck.

BUSINESS MAN: It'll be a pretty buck.

CHORUS: What about us? (Still swaying) Have we not suffered enough?

RICH MAN: Ick! Do something about them. (Pointing to the chorus of victims) Make them disappear. Stat!

Elegy for My Mother

 Get You The Moon | SnØW

Take your asthma medicine.
You don't want to come here.

—Mom (penultimate text)

There is no outside anymore.
No blue sky.

My thoughts choke me.
Every decency inside me struggles to breathe.

I don't know warm from cold.
In all rooms, I get chills.

I see a glare in every glimpse of water,
yet there is no sun.

I think of everything, relentlessly,
but all I want is to think of nothing.

No migraines.
No dizziness.

I should have made of myself
something more than a statue.

My index fingers on my nipples
when I can't sleep.

I seek forgiveness incessantly,
even after it's granted,

in search of an audience
that won't vilify me.

Once, I belonged to my mother.
[Two hearts, and prayer hands] (her final text)

Now, I belong to everyone,
_____ on display.

DISTANT DREAM

Lights Down Low | **MAX**

NICO: You were an English major, right?

ADONIS: Yes. I contain multitudes.

NICO: Then you can be Langston Hughes.

ADONIS: You insult Hughes' legacy. But I'd be honored.

NICO: I'll be Muriel Rukeyser.

ADONIS: I'm so turned on right now.

NICO: It's 1951, you've just published *Montage of a Dream Deferred*, and I've asked you over to discuss poetics.

ADONIS: Very sly of you.

NICO: Go outside, knock on the door. When I let you in, be in character.

(Adonis exits, knocks on door.)

NICO: (Opening the door) Where is the dissident poet?

ADONIS: (Entering) In what brownstone or tenement?

NICO: (Swirling) In what dark room or prison cell?

ADONIS: (Catching Nico) What happens to a dream deferred?

NICO: (Leaning in, as if to kiss Adonis) Time will tell.

ADONIS: (Leaning in) Time will tell.

NICO: (Pulling away) Time...

ADONIS: (Sulking) Nastiest of wardens.

NICO: (To the window) Where is the lover of jazz?

ADONIS: (Following) In what bar room or smoky den?

NICO: (Parting the curtains) In what city will you find him?

ADONIS: (Rubbing her shoulders) When the song is sung...

NICO: (Drooping) Are the blues undone?

ADONIS: (Kissing her neck) Yes, are the blues undone?

NICO: (Turning) The Blues...

ADONIS: (Whispering) A haunted montage.

NICO: (To the bed) Where is the closet communist?

ADONIS: (Following) In what school or college?

NICO: (Lying down) In what ways America's amiss?

ADONIS: (Lying beside her) War, everywhere is war.

NICO: (Facing Adonis) The kiss of death...

ADONIS: (Facing Nico) Without the kiss.

NICO: (Jumping up) I didn't expect...

ADONIS: (Sitting up) This sadness.

NICO: (Back to the window) This quiet.

(Nico climbs out onto the fire escape, and ascends to the roof. Adonis hesitates, then follows her.)

The Snake, the Anus, and the Mouth

Summer | Brock Hampton

The snake is an amazing creature—
unfairly demonized,
you are taught to fear the snake.
But a snake lives in you!
The head of the snake
lives outside the body, sniffing air
for the scent of lavender.
The body of the snake
lives (coiled) inside the body,
like the roots of a tree.
As the tree rises from its roots,
the snake rises from the anus.
The anus is the snake's womb, its cave,
its thermal pocket of protection.
Snake and anus
engage in a dance as ancient as
moon and ocean.
A dance that precedes song.
The song comes after, as a way
to commemorate the dance.
Do not fear the snake!
Say to the snake, Come,
come in my mouth,
give me the words
to taste, that I may swallow
in the moonlight.
Snake, so suddenly effete.

Learning to Leave a Marriage

1.

> an affair
> a job
> a city
> a casino
> a beach
> a hotel
> a lie
> the truth

A speck of truth in a grand opera

All characters are composites of same few people

"But what's the book about?"

Worlds of my daydreaming

A cascade of yearning

"Your yearning is eternal." (She kisses him goodbye.)

2.

Alone in a hotel room:

I come to understand solitude and counterfactuals. The yearning isn't to be carried away by a different life, a different lover. The yearning isn't for a replacement, or parallel universe. The yearning swells, becomes greater than that. The yearning is to hop from one counterfactual to the next. The yearning is to touch them all, to become the one who lives everywhere at the same time, crosses thresholds.

I return from my rendezvous in the afternoon. My absences are less precise in the day.

Sigh. Shower. Sky.

It's easy to look straight ahead, but the neck is designed to do more. I turn intimately toward my shadow.

I know that, repeated, this gaze softens me.

(Fireworks)

(Fireworks)

(Fireworks)

(Fireworks)

(Fireworks)

(Fireworks)

(Fireworks)

(Fireworks)

(Fireworks)

(Fireworks)

(Fireworks)

(Fireworks)

(Fireworks)

(Fireworks)

(Fireworks)

(Fireworks)

look
closer

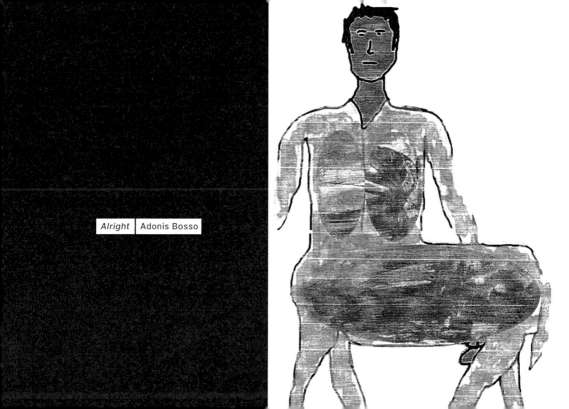

Alright | Adonis Bosso

for example,
when the
concentric waves
in a pond move
away from
the point at
which the stone
fell,
when they move
farther and
farther away and
diminish into
calm, the water
must feel, when
this calm is at-
tained, a kind of
shudder which
is no longer
propagated in
its matter but in
its soul.

JEAN GENET
"Funeral Rites"

POST CARD FROM ANGEL FALLS

Love Language | Kehlani

The Immortal, Magical, Dionysian Act of Inhabiting

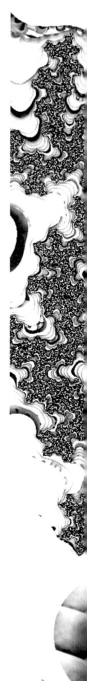

Love Is A Drug | Empress Of

$75 a night, $90.51 with tax,
facing the downtown skyline, the window opens
six inches (no more), what slides in,
a divine wind,
is not a virus, that is the world
jealous of the sun
for its manicured fingers.

— Union
Hotel

I see myself clearly
in the mirror, an orange wall behind me,
I'm here
and I'm not here,
I become a magician, in my solitude
I reflect on my performance,
in one hand: nothing,
in the other hand: a butterfly,
not of this world,
fluttering, then taking off
in particled light,
and me sighing, 'Ah me.'

The
Beautiful
Made
Thing

I live inside a distant dream,
Neruda's "Captain's Verses," from which I read
"Lovely One" to my lovers.
I see myself many times that summer,
framed by the same mirror.
This place must be the eye of the storm.

Love
Bomb

See Adonis

See Adonis falling
that's what it means to die by the sword
but—this is key—that's what they want you to see

    Not him
    in a hot air balloon
    traveling

    along the coast
    parachuting down
    to Solana Beach

See Adonis limping
that's what it means to get beat up
but—remember—that's what they want you to see

    Not his
    former agility
    jumping

    off the pier
    pirouetting through the air
    spinning a basketball on his finger

Because that's what it means to fly

(BULL'S
EYE)

ADONIS' HEART (REPRISE)

I Lost Everything | **Sam Cooke**

ADONIS: (Moaning) My chest! It hurts!

GOD: Alone tonight?

ADONIS: (Writhing) Something's wrong! I'm having a heart attack.

GOD: Perhaps.

ADONIS: My children. Who will take care of them?

GOD: Where's your wife?

ADONIS: Something's not right!

(Adonis twists and turns violently, then stiffens—then his heart bursts through his chest, bouncing off a wall before landing on the floor, leaving a gaping wound in his chest.)

ADONIS: (Freaking) What's that?!

GOD: That's your heart.

ADONIS: (Flushed) What?

GOD: (Picking up Adonis' heart) Heavier than I thought. (He holds it out to Adonis)

ADONIS: (Taking it in his cupped hands) How?

HEART: (To Adonis) You wounded me!

ADONIS: (To his heart) I wounded you?! What about me!?

HEART: You'll manage. But it'll be harder.

ADONIS: Come back.

HEART: No.

ADONIS: Please.

HEART: No.

ADONIS: Then... I'll flush you down the toilet!

HEART: Wait! Just so you know, if you do that, you'll die. For you to stay alive, you must keep me within arm's distance.

ADONIS: You're kidding.

HEART: I'm not. This is real. When you shower, or swim, you must hold me above the water so the both of us don't drown. When you travel, you must put me in a ventilated box, so we don't suffocate. When you have a cold, and are coughing, you must protect me with a mask, because if I catch cold and die, we both die. When it's cold out, you must keep me warm. When it's hot out, you must cool me by fanning me. When you read, or watch a sad film, you'll be incapable of crying. When someone tells a joke, you'll not know how to laugh. Happiness will elude you. Sadness too. Your only measure of fulfillment will be your brain's ability to list things, and check things off a list.

GOD: (To Adonis) It seems like you found yourself another wife.

ADONIS: (To his heart) Impossible! I'll kill myself.

HEART: (To Adonis) Will you?

ADONIS: I will, I swear!

HEART: I'm ready to die. I've proven that...

(Adonis looks around the room. There is blood on the wall where his heart bounced off it. There is blood on the floor where his heart landed. There is God laughing, with blood on his hands. And then there is his heart, talking... Adonis faints. The stage lights turn off.)

(The lights are turned on. Adonis regains consciousness. Ellen is on top of him riding him hard, and choking him. He puts his hands on his chest, relieved to feel his heart beating inside. Ellen is on her period. There's blood all over the sheets, on his belly and thighs. He sees Richard in the corner of the room putting on an astronaut helmet.)

ADONIS: What's he doing here?

ELLEN: I invited him.

(Richard climbs onto the bed and kneels behind Ellen. Adonis can feel Richard's cock as it enters Ellen's ass. Ellen pauses for the insertion, leaning forward and exhaling deeply, before gradually resuming her rocking. Adonis stiffens beneath them as they rock back and forth in rhythm... He comes inside her with a tremendous sigh.)

(Adonis contemplates the tiny corpses on the wall. 'If only a mosquito had the willpower, or self-control, to bite and flee, to not go in for a second or third or fourth bite, it would live a much longer life. But what is the life of a mosquito anyway?! No amount of caution will save it or prolong it. Once it has tasted the blood of a person, it hovers recklessly, as if hypnotized, to bite again and again, until drunk and weighed down by its appetite—an easy mark for a deadly blow. In this way it commits suicide by murder, by greed.' Adonis shivers, because he too is like a mosquito. 'At least they die satiated.' Suddenly, the spots of blood on the wall take on a new hue: that of semen. He smiles deviously as he wipes them with a moist sponge. He's still in a world where people clean up after they fuck.)

The End

Adonis' paternal grandparents,
when they were first married,
lived above a dive bar
in Brooklyn, nearly a century ago.

Adonis was named after his grand uncle
who had polio, and walked with a cane.
He was also one of the fiercest
loan sharks of his day.

His grand uncle loved his father
because his father, aside from being the son
he never had, was fearless,
and ran errands for him with potency.

When Adonis was four years old,
he was kidnapped at the Atlantic Antic.
A woman scooped him up
from a neighbor who was watching him.

Adonis didn't panic or cry.
The woman's face was familiar to him.
He hugged her neck, and twirled her hair
while she walked briskly through the crowd.

She took him to a rooftop in Wyckoff Gardens,
stuck a note inside his pocket,
addressed to his grand uncle, and left him there.
There were no words between them.

There was just sky:
at first, bright, then dimming, then dark.

PEARLY GATES STUDIO

Silhouette of the Pinnacle | Riff Raff, DJ Whoo Kid

GOD: What do you say?

ADONIS: I'm not sure I fully understand.

GOD: We want you in the sequel, we do. But we found a better actor. He's handsome, he's charming, he's funny. He's everything you are, but...better, more, you know...

ADONIS: What's his name?

GOD: Will Peril.

ADONIS: Then what am I doing here?

GOD: The other cast members prefer your cock. (He raises his hands.) I don't understand it either, but they're making a stink about it. So, we figure, we shoot Will for all the acting scenes, and the foreplay and what not, and then you come in for the penetration shots, of which we'll only get close-ups, and then we'll splice them together.

ADONIS: I don't know.

GOD: Put it this way. You're kind of like a stunt double. But instead of doing stunts, you're doing fucking. Vaginal, anal, oral. You know, the holy trinity of porn.

ADONIS: Why can't I do it all?

GOD: We went over this. You're not actor material. You're too...writerly. Listen, we're going to pay you the same as if you were the lead actor. That's very generous of us.

ADONIS: Ok. I guess.

GOD: Great! Sign here. (Adonis signs) Here. (Adonis signs) And here. (Adonis signs)

ADONIS: Where's the Devil?

GOD: He's no longer with us. (God gives Adonis his business card) Our new name and logo.

[An apple tree in bloom.]

(Adonis flips the card.)

[Pearly Gates Studio
God
CEO]

Postcard from Angel Falls

Thinking About Your Body (Louie Vega Dance Ritual Mix | *Josh Molin, Louie Vega*

I enter into the mode of green of each window
I enter into the mode from the beautiful made thing
I enter into the mode when the private face displaces the public face
I enter into the mode while the moon comes into my room
I enter into the mode at the most discrete time
       imperceptible to others
I enter into the mode with the pediment of the sacred
I enter into the mode like an angel falling from heaven
       the arabesque of heaven
I enter into the mode at the feet of Selene
       the image of the glare
            horizon of what is hidden
               or hides in plain view

: Into The Ether

I'm nothing, but a nasal voice,
emanating (at decreasing volume,
for I am falling)
from an angular face.

In film, they'd cast me as a villain,
but I'm happy now.
I'm happy.
Tired, but happy.

I suffered many things,
but I don't want to list them,
which would be a type of bragging,
because to brag would be to win at suffering.

And to win at suffering,
one would have to be suffering now.
I'm done with suffering.
I'm happy.

Yes, occasionally I have a terrible
migraine, or bout of nausea.
I overcome these attacks
through my indulgences.

Or, one could argue (as God has!),
by cheapening my appetite.

SELENE AS MUSE MAGNIFIQUE

Love You Like A Love Song | Selena Gomez & The Scene

(The muse Narrator

The muse MC

The muse Curator

The muse DJ

The muse Director

The muse Filmmaker

The muse Choreographer

The muse Manager

The muse Conductor

The muse Composer

The muse Maestro

The muse Contralto

The muse Hydra

The muse God

The muse Devil

The muse Archangel

The muse Myth

The muse Supreme

The muse Mermaid

The muse Siren

The muse Star, North

The muse Theorist

The muse Genius

The muse Operator, Smooth

The muse Synthesizer

The muse Gymnast

The muse Acrobat

The muse Architect

The muse Painter

The muse Cartographer

The muse Wizard

The muse Teller, Fortune

The muse Witch

The muse Cocaine

The muse Alien

The muse Mystic, Natural

The muse Hero

The muse Antihero

The muse Martyr

The muse Phoenix

The muse Fire

The muse Fiend

The muse Addict

The muse Dealer, Drug

The muse Dealer, Card

The muse Pilot

The muse Captain

The muse Astronaut

The muse Diver

The muse Lightning

The muse Thunder

The muse Season, Hurricane

The muse Season, Monsoon

The muse Wave, Tidal

The muse Earthquake

The muse Gravity

The muse Magnet

The muse Force, Weak

The muse Force, Strong

The muse Orgasm, Double)

ADONIS: (Postcoital) Selene est un magnifique l'amant.

Elegy for Adonis

Flower (Girly-Sound Version) | Liz Phair

You fuck,
writing your own epitaph:

> (in order of manifestation)
> son,
> brother,
> father,
> husband,
> false poet,
> lover,
> revived poet,
> and for 'poet' you can substitute 'friend' as well

Fuck you
for your metamorphosis,
for learning how to fly
and leaving those who loved you behind.
As a child
you were loved more than you loved.
As a man
you loved more than you were loved.
This liberated you.
As a lover
you loved until your love unbound
your human form.
Your last words:

> When I swim, I feel free.
> The water kisses me all over.

You down with FFF (yeah, you know me), you down with FFF (yeah, you know me)
You down with FFF (yeah, you know me), who's down with FFF (every last author)
You down with FFF (yeah, you know me), you down with FFF (yeah, you know me)
You down with FFF (yeah, you know me), who's down with FFF (all my authors)

FFF, how can I define it	T
I'll take you through each iteration	h
To have you all revising and editing	e
Until you achieve the final, final, final version	
	L
First F is for Final, Second F is for Final	a
Third F, well, that's the final, Final	s
The final stroke, the finishing touch	t
The embalming of the work for public display	
	P
It's sort of like a wedding after the engagement party	u
It's sort of like a book after the galley proof	r
It's three letters of profound communication, like XXX	g
You get the picture without the genuflection	e
As an end goal, it should motivate you to do better	o
To remind you, first thought is not best thought	f
Or even a fully developed thought	
Worthy of anything except more thought	A
	d
So script it, not once, not twice, but thrice	o
Because the asking price is not the same as the purchase price	n
And you can put that on ice	i
And ship it to paradise with a garnish of edelweiss	s

You down with FFF (yeah, you know me), you down with FFF (yeah, you know me)
You down with FFF (yeah, you know me), who's down with FFF (every last author)
You down with FFF (yeah, you know me), you down with FFF (yeah, you know me)
You down with FFF (yeah, you know me), who's down with FFF (all my authors)

STAY

SELENE: I saw myself, my future self, in his smile and eyes, and I was moved—surprised—to see myself fabulously androgynous. Then he jumped.

1. Stay	Rihanna, Mikky Ekko	4:00
2. Shape of You	Ed Sheeran	3:53
3. My Angel	Horace Andy	2:54
4. Lights Down Low	MAX	3:43
5. Something Just Like This	The Chainsmokers, Coldplay	4:06
6. Alive	Krewella	4:50
7. Get on Top	Tim Buckley	6:32
8. You Know How to Make Me Feel so Good	Susan Cadogan	5:01
9. Dive In	Trey Songz	4:12
10. Love You Like A Love Song	Selena Gomez & The Scene	3:08
11. L-O-V-E – Long Version	Joss Stone	2:48
12. Love U Better	Victoria Monét	3:51
13. PILLOWTALK	ZAYN	3:22
14. No Judgement	Niall Horan	2:55
15. Stay	**Zedd, Alessia Cara**	**3:29**
16. Under Your Spell	Desire	4:55
17. I Want Your Love	Chromatics	6:40

1hr 10m

ALL NIGHT

SELENE: But Adonis loves Thaïs! Adonis loves Nico! Adonis loves me! Adonis loves all his lovers—husbands and wives be damned! Religious and moral institutions be damned!

1. Dopamine	BØRNS	3:44
2. Get You The Moon	Kina, Snøw	2:58
3. Moonage Daydream	David Bowie	4:39
4. All Night	**Bree Runway**	**3:38**
5. 77	Kaivon, Kini Solana	4:08
6. I Want You	Erykah Badu	10:52
7. Sugar on My Tongue	Talking Heads	2:36
8. Levitating	Dua Lipa, DaBaby	3:22
9. My Neck, My Back (Lick It)	Khia	3:42
10. The Sixth Night: Waking	Muriel Rukeyser	0:24
11. Touch Me	Victoria Monét, Kehlani	3:07
12. moonlight	dhruv	2:38
13. I'm The Man, That Will Find You	Connan Mockasin	5:01
14. All About U	Rai-Elle	2:55
15. You	Yellow Days	4:05
16. Aquarius/Let The Sunshine In	The 5th Dimension	4:48
17. All Night – Unfinished	Jai Paul	3:12

1hr 6m

IF 6 WAS 9

SELENE: Unlike most centaurs, Adonis yearned to be a horse fully. Now that he is only a floating head (a watercolor), he slips off the page.

1. Do I Move You?	Nina Simone	2:44
2. You Know I'm No Good	Amy Winehouse	4:16
3. Nannou (EP Version)	Aphex Twin	4:15
4. If 6 Was 9	Jimi Hendrix	5:34
5. Numb	Portishead	3:57
6. Lost and Lookin'	Sam Cooke	2:11
7. Hurt	Johnny Cash	3:36
8. Don't Let Me Be Misunderstood	Nina Simone	2:46
9. Talkin'	Bob Marley & Dermot Hussey	1:51
10. I Shot the Sheriff	Bob Marley & The Wailers	7:12
11. Oh Shooter	Robin Thicke	4:36
12. I Lost Everything	Sam Cooke	3:23
13. Bitter	Meshell Ndegeocello	4:15
14. The Piano Has Been Drinking (Not Me)	Tom Waits	3:40
15. Strangelove	Depeche Mode	4:54
16. Silhouette of the Pinnacle	Riff Raff, DJ Whoo Kid	3:53
17. Coney Island Winter	Garland Jeffreys	3:46

1hr 6m

HONEY MAN

SELENE: Adonis spent his life writing poems from the nadir of a sexual addiction—or abjection. Adonis, of himself: 'I'm me. Ah me.' And: 'I'm me. Ravish me.'

1. Legend In His Own Mind	Gil Scott-Heron	3:40
2. Make It Fast, Make It Slow	Rob	5:25
3. Honey Man	Tim Buckley	4:11
4. He Knows a Lot of Good Women	Love	3:15
5. Mr. Sexy Man	Nellie Tiger Travis	4:09
6. The Man Who Couldn't Afford to Orgy	John Cale	4:33
7. Pony	Ginuwine	4:11
8. Feelin' Lovely	Connan Mockasin, Devonté Hynes	3:51
9. Love Is A Drug	Empress Of	2:39
10. Disco Man	Remi Wolf	3:11
11. Company	Tinashe	3:39
12. Serial Lover	Kehlani	2:25
13. Fuckboy	BAUM	3:00
14. Fancy Man	Devendra Banhart	2:59
15. I Just Wanna Lay Around All Day In Bed With You	The Coup	5:15
16. Flower (Girly-Sound Version)	Liz Phair	2:47
17. O.P.P	Naughty By Nature	4:30

1h 3m

DISTANT DREAM (NICO'S PLAYLIST)

ADONIS: The two nuclei of my life are the bedroom—a stage for fucking—and the toilet. In these spaces, which are as much moments as spaces, I transcend my disillusion... I miss being naked with you in a hotel room.

1. Masquerade	Clan of Xymox	3:54
2. Cherry-coloured Funk	Cocteau Twins	3:12
3. The Line	Mood Rings	3:23
4. Distant Dream	John Carpenter	3:51
5. Alles ist gut	PA Sports	3:56
6. Heartbeats (Live)	The Knife	4:21
7. A Real Hero	College & Electric Youth	4:27
8. Pretender	Black Marble	3:22
9. Crimewave (Crystal Castles Vs.) (David Wolf Edit)	HEALTH	2:40
10. Angel of the Morning	Juice Newton	4:14
11. Nights in White Satin (Single Version)	The Moody Blues	4:24
12. Please Don't Touch (The Golden Filter Remix)	Polly Scattergood, The Golden Filter	6:25
13. A Day	Clan of Xymox	6:40
14. End of the World	Anika	2:56
15. Cry in the Wind	Clan of Xymox	5:16
16. Love Bomb	N.E.R.D	4:35
17. Huit octobre 1971	Cortex	4:26

1h 12 m

SUMMERTIME

SELENE: I met him the first time on a weekday afternoon. I didn't think he was going to show up. It was the summer of the grand dispersal, at the beginning of the quote-unquote emergence.

1. Feels Like Summer	Childish Gambino	4:56
2. Summer 2020	Jhené Aiko	3:15
3. SUMMER	BROCKHAMPTON	3:24
4. Summertime	Louis Armstrong, Ella Fitzgerald	4:57
5. LAVENDER	Dounia	2:18
6. Eternity	Noah Collette, Sonia Tavik, Kenndoe	3:21
7. Kiss U Right Now	Duckwrth	3:14
8. Tell Me	NEIL FRANCES, The Undercover Dream Lovers	3:17
9. I'll Be There For You/You're All I Need	Method Man, Mary J. Blige	3:40
10. Come Over	Ce'Cile, ZJ Chrome	3:22
11. Soul Control	Jessie Ware	3:59
12. Summertime	**Stick Figure, Citizen Cope**	**3:58**
13. Anda Jaleo	Paco de Lucía, Andres Batista, Manolo Sanlucar	2:25
14. 500 Days of Summer	Grady	1:53
15. Go To Town	Doja Cat	3:37
16. Jaguar	Victoria Monét	3:30
17. Move Like This	Ric Wilson, Terrace Martin	4:04

59m

BEAUTIFUL (BIRTHDAY SUITE)

SELENE: His hands were soft, as if he never touched anything rough or ragged. His fingernails were meticulously manicured. His skin was silky, and smelled of lavender. He had a feminine sensibility, with the physique of a man, the body of a swimmer—long torso, broad shoulders, thin waist, potent thighs, and a cock that bent slightly to the left. There was a sadness to his lovemaking, at a depth deeper than what I was accustomed to. He described himself as a follower in the bed. And so, I pegged him properly!

1. Baby	Donnie & Joe Emerson	4:09
2. American Money	BØRNS	4:20
3. Pussy Is God	King Princess	3:25
4. Good Pussy	Alia Kadir	3:02
5. I'll Wait	Kygo, Sasha Alex Sloan	3:34
6. Beautiful	Bazzi	2:57
7. Tonight You Might	Synthia, Lady Wray	3:51
8. Beautiful Escape	Tom Misch, Zak Abel	4:36
9. Beautiful	Qveen Herby	3:23
10. What's Your Pleasure?	Jessie Ware	4:37
11. disco tits	Tove Lo	3:43
12. Gemini	Knox Fortune	3:02
13. Mysterium Tremendum	Christopher Young	1:40
14. Birthday Suit	Kesha	2:55
15. Birthday Sex	Jeremih	3:45
16. I Wanna Roll With You	Connan Mockasin	5:44
17. Hit the Back	King Princess	3:23

1hr 2m

ALL MY LOVERS

ADONIS: Selene, you're my sultry narrator. In your mouth, my name is a benediction.

1. All My Lovers	Black Tape For A Blue Girl	4:01
2. Thinking About Your Body (Louie Vega Dance Ritual Mix)	Josh Milan, Louie Vega	11:10
3. No Silhouette	DPR IAN	2:28
4. FALLING	Che Ecru	2:13
5. Love Language	Kehlani	3:32
6. Alright	Adonis Bosso	3:18
7. One And Four (AKA Mr. Day)	John Coltrane	7:36
8. Woman Is a Word	Empress Of	3:16
9. You Don't Love Me (No, No, No) – Extended Mix	Dawn Penn	4:37
10. Yannis and the Dragon	Christodoulos Halaris	6:57
11. Softness As A Weapon	Kindness	5:08
12. We Should Be Together	Pia Mia	3:43
13. Motorbike	Leon Bridges	3:08
14. Licking An Orchid	Yves Tumor, James K	4:37
15. Don't Wait Up	Oh He Dead	4:10
16. I'm Good, I'm Gone	Lykke Li	3:08
17. I'm Gonna Do My Thing	Royal Deluxe	3:09

1h 16m

Marquee

(((Gasp)))

Applause
Laughter

Standing Oral	*Missionary*	*Rope Bondage*
Queening	*69*	*Spooning*
Butterfly	*Doggy Style*	*Double Penetration*

ADULT THEATER

VIP ROOMS   PAY-PER-VIEW

WARNING!
THESE SCENES ARE EXPLICIT

| *I Want Your Love* | Chromatics |

Cosmos

Gasp
(((Applause)))
Laughter

Cancer	Leo	Taurus
Gemini	Libra	Aquarius
Sagittarius	Aries	Scorpio

VIRGO VS. CAPRICORN
WITH PISCES AS HOST

SUNSET   SUNRISE

WATERFALL
INTO LAKE

I'll Wait	Kygo, Sasha Alex Sloan

A DUSTING

Coney Island Winter | Garland Jeffreys

(Selene is burning Adonis' books in a pot on the stove. She stirs the fire with a long spoon until it burns out. Then she carefully gathers all the ashes into a coffee tin. She places the tin next to a collage Adonis had made for her.)

SELENE: (To the collage) I'll keep you. (She covers the tin and packs it into a beach bag. Then, she exits.)

> Interior shot: Train station
> Exterior shot: Street

(Selene emerges from the station. The sky is gray. There are very few people outside. The Cyclone is idle. She walks to the boardwalk, then to the pier, then to the end of the pier, to its cross. There are a few fishermen who barely acknowledge her. She measures the wind, then settles in the Eastern corner.)

SELENE: (Opening the tin) Dear Universe, thank you for my times with Adonis. And thank you for my life, in general. For all my blessings. For all my lovers.

(She cups some ashes into her palm, extends her arm over the railing and opens her hand. The wind swirls the ashes into an almost human figure—a man pirouetting! Then the air dissolves the ashes, and the ocean cushions their fall. She empties out the tin one handful at a time. Each time she sees a person dance in the wind before disappearing.)

SELENE: See Adonis falling... Amen.

(She lingers for a moment, wiping her hands with a moist towelette. It starts snowing.)

(Adonis lays down on a bed...The ceiling and walls of the room melt away.
A double-decker bus pulls up and parks beside his bed.

Scantily clad women emerge from the bus and gawk at him.
One woman leans over him, her breasts brushing against his stomach.
One leans over him, resting her breasts on his face.

They all lean over him, climb on top of him, push him
further down into the mattress. His arousal turns to panic.
He tries to push them off, to get up, but he is overwhelmed.
He can't breathe. Everything goes dark.

In that darkness he can feel himself leaving his body.
He wakes up in a hotel room. Selene is there. He has a lopsided
headache, and his vision is blurry, as if looking underwater.
"I blacked out," he says. The sound of his own voice feels
muffled, disconnected. "I know. I'm here," Selene says, her
speech emanating from her edges.

"Water," she says, handing him a glass. He feels
another surge of darkness coming. He feels shame he's
with Selene, and not his children. He feels regret for
burdening her with nursing him. He worries his end
will blemish her youth.

The darkness is upon him. "Hold this," he
returns the glass. The darkness overtakes
him, incrementally but fiercely. It doesn't
so much carry him away as it dissolves him,
consumes him, digests him.)

Complete List of Characters

(in alphabetical order)

Adonis (language endowed)

Announcer (voice)

Astronaut

Bartender

Broumas

Business Man

Cheetah (Selene's spirit animal)

Child 1

Child 2

Cock (speaking)

Cormorant (Adonis' spirit animal)

Dermot Hussey

Devil

Ellen (half of Two Beasts)

Enzo

First Responders

God

Heart (speaking)

HR Woman

Husband (a young Adonis)

Lady in Fine Hat

Lorca

Madam Boss

Mail Man

Marley

Milk Man

MRI Technician

Narrator (silhouette and voice)

Nico

Nurse

Olivia

Paperboy

Parishioners

Index of Poems

Green Of Each Window:

Crystalline Green:

Index of Images

I see you

I see you
seeing me